A DARK BREED

THE MONSTERS & MAYHEM COLLECTION
BOOK ONE

PATRICK MCNULTY

THE MINISTRY OF THE WRAITH PRESS

~

For Seth Wimmer, an amazing writer and a better friend.

Thanks for everything.

~

CHAPTER
ONE

Desperate, guttural shrieks erupted from the plastic baby monitor. The four tiny bulbs set into the base flashed in the dark and painted the walls of the tiny bedroom with a splash of garish red light.

Aching, agonizing screams ripped through the thin veil of sleep covering Professor Harry Marks and he awoke with a jolt. He blinked, still dazed, halfway between awake and dreaming to find his bedroom painted in blood.

A scream bubbled to his lips. He blinked again, clearing the hazy film of sleep. His eyes flicked madly left and right across the room as he slowly realized...*no*...no, the room was not covered in blood. It was only light. Red light from the monitor.

The screaming waned for a moment, its volume dipping below excruciating, and the indicator lights on the baby monitor went dark. But in that pocket of silence the professor heard something else. Something even more troubling. A dull tone. Incessant and steady. An alarm was ringing inside the bunker.

For a moment he was trapped there, where he was, propped up on his right elbow, frozen in place. His quick breaths barely visible, smoking in the frigid air and forming a halo around his head that smelled faintly of old whiskey and stale cigarettes.

He had forgotten to fill the generator again before he went to sleep. The temperature inside the cabin was, if he were to guess, a few degrees below freezing. Outside the weather had turned again with a new storm system roaring in from eastern Canada.

He knew about this. He should have been more prepared.

His head ached from the whiskey and he had his answer. He could hear the pellets of ice hit the narrow window above his bed. Tiny claws tapping on the glass.

The alarm continued its call through the baby monitor.

He had to get up.

He had to move.

But his eyes were pinned to the pale red smear of the baby monitor. Only one red bulb was lit now. Above and beyond the steady *beep...beep...beep...*of the alarm a low murmuring leaked from the tinny speaker, a dense whispering that he could never hope to decipher.

Who was she talking to?

Was it him?

Did she know he could hear her?

His elbow started to ache and the warmth of the bed

beneath the thick down comforters was beginning to bleed away. He could feel the cold on his nose at first. He always felt it there. After so many bouts of frostbite over the years it was his canary in the coal mine. Next the bitter cold would settle into his cheeks below his eyes, sinking into his flesh, turning his pale pink skin the color of wet cement. He had to get moving. He had to get to the bunker.

The alarm. What was happening?

He should not be hearing the low repeating tone. It doesn't matter. It's happening. This is not a test. He needed to quiet the alarm and then get the generator started and warm up the cabin before the —

The woman screamed again and the tiny red bulbs of light exploded into the bedroom throwing ghastly shadows of crooked, dangerous things across the rough timber walls.

He felt a pain in the center of his chest as if she had reached through the monitor and wrapped her long, cold fingers around his heart in an icy fist. He felt his core temperature drop like a stone. His spine turned to ice as his primal, lizard brain ran through its bizarre checklist deciding whether to fight or flee.

Foreign words built of hate and ancient curses spiced with sharp electronic crackles and the hiss of static, roared through the whining speakers that were never designed to broadcast this volume of threat.

.   .   .

Harry could feel himself holding his breath as his heart hammered against his ribs like a frightened bird. And then, just as quickly as it had come, the woman fell silent. The red lights dimmed, the twitching shadows melted back into the night and the bedroom was plunged back into darkness.

Only the steady *beep...beep...beep* of the alarm filtered through the static.

In the relative silence the professor seized the opportunity and swept back the covers. He winced as the bracing air of the cabin washed over his skinny frame. A brushfire of goosebumps spread across his skin as he swung his legs over the side of the bed.

With his bare feet on the floor he could reach the baby monitor he had set up on the bedside table. His hand was shaking as he reached out and switched the monitor off. The last red indicator light faded and died and he let out a shuddering breath.

Without the noise of the monitor, silence flooded into the bedroom and smothered the room in a heavy stillness that rang in his ears.

Pale moonlight spilled through the window above the bed and limned the overstuffed chair piled high with his clothes, and transformed the clouds of his breath into ghostly white spectres that twisted and writhed before they disappeared into the dark.

With his breathing slowed and his heart rate returning to its normal clip, he reached for the battery powered lantern and found that his hand was no longer shaking. There was a sharp click that sounded like a gunshot in the quiet space and then light, clean and white, flooded his bedroom. There were no pictures of family and friends on the walls. No artwork. The cabin wasn't a weekend getaway. It was basecamp. A headquarters.

He finger combed the wild strands of long grey hair that stood out straight from his tiny skull as if they were trying to escape during the night and pushed himself up from the bed. The arthritis that he had decided to ignore had continued to advance across the landscape of his body, creeping into his bones and rusting the joints of his hips and back. In the cold, dry weather his knuckles swelled to the size of barnacles transforming his hands into painfully formed claws.

The wind howled somewhere close, a living thing just outside the walls that hurled a fistful of ice pellets at the bedroom window, rattling the glass in the frame.

Harry's rough bare feet brushed across the hardwood boards to the chair buried under a pile of clothes. Once there he grabbed a pair of jeans, a hooded blue sweatshirt emblazoned with UCLA across the chest and a bundle of thick wool socks. He sat on the edge of the bed and winced as he went through the mechanics of stretching, bending over, and dressing himself, feeling every day of his sixty-seven years.

Dressed, he stood, and tightened the belt around his waist. He noticed he was using the last hole in the leather belt and the jeans he wore still threatened to slip down over his bony hips.

He knew he had lost more weight in the last two

months, but he didn't think it was that bad. That far gone.

When did that happen?

He thought about the last time he had something to eat that wasn't a handful of trail mix or ramen noodles and he came up empty.

HE SHUFFLED out of the bedroom carrying the lantern and turned right down the hall. He stopped in the bathroom and studied himself in the mirror. A silver halo of hair surrounded his angular face covered in at least three days of stubbly white beard. His blue eyes were still bright, but they had faded to the color of denim sometime during the last twenty years or so. The weight loss, and the drinking accompanied by a diet typical of a poor college student left his face looking skeletal, his eyes ringed with purple bags the color of old bruises.

He scraped a hand down his face and shook his head. He looked like shit and there was no getting around that. This whole ordeal had taken a lot more out of him than he would admit, but he would be damned if he was gonna call that smug sonofabitch back in New York for an extension. He was old and decrepit, but he would finish the book on time. He was so close. He just had to take better care of himself. Maybe get down the mountain for a real meal, not some reheated, rehydrated bag of garbage that smelled like shit and tasted worse. More sleep. Better food. Less whiskey. That was all he needed. Balance.

With the wispy threads of a plan in place he left the bathroom and headed down the hall to the main open concept living area of the cabin. He set the lantern down on the large hand carved wooden desk he had brought from Denver. The harsh light illuminated his laptop surrounded by a stash of newspaper clippings, a sketchbook and a tragically empty bottle of Bushmills. His last bottle.

The plan he had just decided to employ in order to improve his well being evaporated quicker than water on a hot skillet and his mouth watered for even a single sip.

God, he could use a drink right now.

Harry lifted the empty bottle and saw a few drops hidden at the bottom and thought of tipping it back, what could it hurt?

A layer of frost coated the glass and he remembered why he was going out in the cold at this hour. He had gotten drunk as usual last night and forgot to restart the generator. He was losing control.

Then he thought of the woman.

And her screaming.

And the alarm.

Jesus, the alarm.

It was all too much.

He needed to focus. He needed to be sharp.

They had found him, and they were coming.

CHAPTER

TWO

Harry set the bottle down and moved to the front door where he pulled his heavy parka from the peg and slipped his arms into the sleeves. The parka smelled of smoke. Bonfires, cigars, cigarettes and even the smoke of a large tent fire he had helped extinguish while in the mountains of Nepal. The parka had been torn and ripped over the years and repaired with patches and fabrics from around the world, but the scent of smoke remained.

The parka smelled of adventure and reminded him of an earlier time when his body didn't feel like it was on the verge of collapse. A time when he was strong and capable. He breathed in the musty odor of the coat and felt the corners of his mouth twitch into a smile.

He dug his right hand into the pocket of his parka and retrieved a small but powerful flashlight. He pressed the power button to check if it still worked. Satisfied, he stuffed it back into his pocket.

Dressed in boots, gloves and a wool toque, Professor Harry Marks unlocked the deadbolt on the cabin's front door. Immediately the door swung inward, powered by the freezing gust that seemed to be lying in wait, desperate to bully its way inside.

Harry lowered his head as the ice riding on the wind needled his face as he stepped into the wailing wind, and dragged the door closed behind him. He heard the click of the lock engaging and then turned his attention to the driveway where his aging Ford F-150 sat glistening, coated in a thin layer of ice and snow.

Harry did his best to keep his head down, shielding his face from the wind, but there was nowhere to hide. His cheeks burned with cold as he trudged toward the tree line, finding the well worn path through the woods mostly by muscle memory.

Behind the screen of the tall swaying pines the wind was less horrific, even though Harry didn't exactly feel relaxed moving through the maze of towering trees as they creaked and groaned bending impossibly back and forth in the gale force winds.

It was darker here, away from the weak light of the moon, and he dug out his flashlight. The bright white beam cut through the gloom and lit up the forest around him. He swept the beam up ahead and found the door of his custom made bunker built against the side of the rock face that rose up past the tops of the pines and out of view.

The bunker was fashioned from the same rough timbers used to build the cabin and was twelve feet wide, eight feet tall and sported a single entrance and no windows.

Harry moved slowly forward, stumbling only once when his boot caught on a root hidden beneath the snow. He swore in the dark, and his words frosted the air around his head.

Ten feet away from the only entrance, a steel door painted in slashes of greens and browns to blend into the landscape swam into view. Harry had to remove his gloves to retrieve his ring of keys and in those sparse moments the freezing air knifed into his flesh and threatened to cripple his hands.

He worked quickly, first finding the right key on the ring festooned with keys, one usually dedicated to high school janitors, and then unlocking the two padlocks that secured the steel door. Harry lost his grip on the first padlock and the metal clanked against the steel, igniting a wretched wail from inside. The sound bore into his ears and Harry saw that his fingers were shaking as he carefully inserted the right key and twisted.

He slipped the lock into his coat pocket and went to work on the second as the woman inside continued to shriek. A moment later the second lock was removed and then Harry thankfully slipped his gloves back on to remove the sliding bolts. With the bolts retracted he gripped the fixed vertical handle on the metal door with both gloved hands and pulled backward and stepped into the shrieking darkness.

CHAPTER

THREE

The dark inside the bunker was alive with so many sounds. So many awful noises that for a second Harry's head felt dizzy and a wave of nausea swept over him. He secured the door behind him and then fumbled for the light switch and missed.

The woman's feverish screaming, the steady beeping of alarms and the constant metallic clanking as the woman shook the cell door in its frame was enough to send shards of glass through his brain.

He needed a minute. Even a second. With his back against the metal door he closed his eyes and focused on his breathing. He needed to focus, but the hangover and the violent cacophony of noise drove logical, rational thought from his mind.

Focus.

The alarm.

Harry opened his eyes and with his right hand he

found the light switch and immediately the bunker was flooded with soft white light.

The cage sat near the original entrance to the mining tunnel. It was ten feet square and constructed of metal panels consisting of six vertical metal bars each. The result was a freestanding prison cell with a single fortified entry door that was secured with a padlock.

It was warmer in the bunker than the outside with the dedicated generator running a bank of electric heaters, but not by much. It was comfortable, but it certainly wasn't warm. At least not to Harry.

The woman stood stock still, the too big peasant dress of yellowing cotton hung from her thin frame. Her long, greasy, black hair hung in sweaty tangles covering most of her face, but he still saw the dark wet buttons of her eyes glaring out at him. Pinpricks of light sparked off their glossy surface. She gripped the bars of the door and stared at him, tracking his every movement with only her eyes.

Like a predator, he thought.

She was no longer screaming. She was whispering. Low and secret, something only she could hear.

Her stink was palpable. Days of old sweat and unwashed flesh mixed with the puddles of piss and piles of shit the woman deposited on the floor of the cell brought a train of bile rushing up Harry's throat.

The last time he was here he had strung a veritable forest of pine scented air fresheners around the tiny space, but they were woefully inefficient. Her stink filled the room in a haze that left a film on his skin. His first order of business after silencing the alarm was to take a shower and wash the smell of her away.

He covered his mouth with his gloved hand and pushed off from the door to a metal desk that sat in the far corner. He took a seat in the rolling desk chair and studied the black screens of the dual computer monitors.

He touched the mouse and the screens flickered to life. The monitor on the left displayed the status of what he had labeled UV Fence number 1 through 4. The monitor on the right was split into four quadrants. Each quadrant showed the view from four separate night vision cameras that were mounted along the length of the abandoned mining tunnel, that extended from the bunker into the mountain.

The word ALARM flashed across the part of the screen pertaining to UV FENCE #4. He used the mouse and with a click, silenced the alarm. He studied the screen and saw that UV FENCE #4 was showing OFFLINE. He frowned.

He had fortified the length of mining tunnel himself, as much as he could, to prevent any damage to his equipment, but things happened. The mountain was not a static thing. The earth shook from time to time and rocks fell. But if a rock had come loose and damaged his equipment he would expect it to be *damaged*. Not completely offline. Not destroyed.

Suddenly an alarm sounded flashing big and bright across the screen. The alarm was coming from UV FENCE #3.

What the hell?

He switched his focus to the monitor on the right and checked every view. The far end of the tunnel was dark without the UV light fence, but the rest of the tunnel was lit. He saw a flicker of motion on the screen and leaned closer to the monitor.

No.

Something moved at the edge of the camera's range. Something dark and big and fast.

The alarm sounded again and Harry saw that UV FENCE #3 was losing power.

Fast.

And along with it, its functionality...*85%...77%...56%...*

His gaze flicked back to the video feeds again and he saw a shape dart through the semi-dark. Was it...Harry squinted...*was it throwing something?*

Rocks.

Rocks the size of basketballs sailed out of the dark and smashed into the small metal transformer boxes that powered UV FENCE #3.

Holy shit.

Behind him the woman had begun to scream. A high wailing shriek that sounded more like a war cry than a plea for help. Harry's head snapped toward her and he found that she had silently changed position. No longer was she at the cell door. Now, she was pressed against the wall closest to the opening of the tunnel. Her arms outstretched through the bars, her long black fingertips reaching out toward the darkness as her ancient language spilled from her cracked lips in a steady stream of encouragement.

They were coming for her.

They were coming for you, too. Harry's mind whispered.

The soft pink that had just begun to color his cheeks quickly bled away and he found himself, once again, frozen by fear.

They were coming.

They were here. His mind corrected.

He couldn't move. He couldn't think. It was all right, he told himself. Two more UV systems were still in place. Whatever was damaging the first two he could stop. There were fail safes. He tried to think but the woman had begun to shriek again, somehow reaching an ear-splitting volume he didn't believe humanly possible.

It was hard to think. Hard to concentrate. That and the hangover and the lack of sleep, Harry felt his hands ball into fists. The woman screamed louder and louder and shook the metal wall of the cell, aiming her tirade at the entrance to the ancient mining tunnel.

Rage built up inside the old professor, a molten hot frustration that powered him out of the desk chair, across the floor and to the long, rectangular gun safe he had bolted to the wall. He fished out the ring of keys and found the right one, stabbing it into the lock, all the while keeping one eye on the monitor where UV FENCE #3 was now reading at 23% and falling.

He yanked open the door to the gun safe and pulled

out a Mossberg pump-action shotgun already affixed with a thin UV flashlight.

CHAPTER

FOUR

Armed with the shotgun Harry switched on the attached UV light and swept the beam over the bars of the cage. The purple light splashed across the woman's flesh eliciting a sharp squeal of pain. The woman spun and danced away from the beam, curling into a ball behind the filthy cot, the only other item in her cell. After a moment, Harry aimed the light elsewhere but the woman continued to glare at him, snarling and spitting curses in her foreign language.

The corners of Harry's mouth twitched into a smile. It felt good to see her cowering. Even just to shut her up for a second.

"That's right, bitch." He muttered. "Be right back."

He was in charge here.

She was the savage, scared of a little bright light. He turned back to the gun cabinet and grabbed handfuls of shells from a box on a shelf and stuffed his pockets full.

This was not how he imagined this to go. Not at all.

But boundaries had to be placed. Protocols established. He was not about to be bullied. He fed the shells into the loading port, clicking each one into place until it was full and then racked one into the barrel.

He moved back to the control panel and checked the status.

UV FENCE #3 had gone completely offline and UV FENCE #2 was beginning to fade, already down to 63%.

The greasy layer of sweat coating Harry's body was beginning to freeze.

This was really happening.

He saw that the woman had shifted along the rear wall of the cage, dirty hands clasped around the bars. Her voice a pleading misery toward the open entrance. Desperate still, but definitely not as vicious. She was communicating with whatever was damaging his equipment, that much was clear.

He had to do something.

Quick.

In the law of the jungle he had to assert his dominance and he had to do it with swift and brutal violence. It was the universal language respected by all. Since the beginning of time the strongest made the rules and so it was written. He gripped the heavy shotgun in his hands and felt his heart shudder for a beat in his chest. He had the weapons. He was smarter. This could only end one way.

He left the computer terminals and strode past the screaming woman who clung to the cage wall. He smashed the butt of his shotgun at the bars, aiming at the fingers of her left hand. But she was too fast. He struck nothing but steel and succeeding in only making a clanking sound that shook the metal cage. The filthy, half-naked woman skipped backward and hissed at him, spewing more venomous words, her tangled black hair whipped around her head and stuck to her bare skin.

She stuck a crooked index finger out at him and hissed a slew of consonants and vowels that Harry innately knew was a curse, a threat and a death warrant all rolled into one. He didn't have to know what it meant for him to know that if it weren't for the metal cage between them, she would kill him, or die trying.

The computer terminal whined again as UV FENCE #2's operational strength dropped below 10%.

He was lucky to have trapped the woman, he didn't believe he would have enough luck to stop whatever else was coming. He would have to kill them before they did any more real damage. He would shoot them if he had to, and then repair his UV systems. Or move. More likely move with the woman to a safer place, somewhere they couldn't hear her screaming in order to continue his study.

Yes, the thought of moving far away from this mountain command center felt right. He had spent too many cold, lonely nights at the top of the world. He would start packing today. He could be gone by the end of the week. The realization of a plan coming together, however flimsy, put a bounce in his step.

But first, he would have to deal with the problem in the tunnel.

Harry moved to the rear of the bunker and peered around the left side of the widened mining tunnel entrance. His memory returned to the first time he set eyes on the entrance. He had found it after three months of careful research. After three months of freezing cold nights waiting and watching, setting up trail cameras and painstakingly examining the captured data, of poring over days and weeks of footage.

Only Harry knew what it truly was.

But soon the world would know its value. Once his book was finished the entire world would discover a brave new world. A world Harry hoped to eventually explore.

But not today.

The entryway to the mine was fitted with a steel door with sliding metal bolts identical to the outer door of the bunker. For a moment he thought about abandoning the UV fence. Let them have it. He could lock the door and be done with it. They would never be able to get through that. A solid steel door with locking bolts drilled into the rock face. He didn't care how strong they thought they were. It was called a *fail safe* for a reason.

He gripped his shotgun and felt the pulse of pain in his palsied hands and thought about it. Seriously. It would be so easy. Swing the heavy thing closed and forget about it. He didn't pay for the UV fence, what did he care.

But he was smarter than to think the attack would end there. When he researched the mine he knew there was, at the time of the decommissioning, thirty-three documented entrances scattered around the mountain.

Thirty-three.

And those were only the ones they knew about. Thirty-three represented only the entrances that were commercially viable. Harry believed there were at least double that number. He had just dug out one of them and laid down a welcome mat.

He heard his father's voice whisper in the dark, '*Be careful what you wish for Harry.*'

Harry peeked around the corner as bits of rock and clouds of dust fell from the stones precariously held in place above his head by new and ancient beams. He could see the purple glow of UV FENCE #1 twenty-seven feet further down the tunnel. It was still intact. Still 100% operational. For now.

Listening at the corner of the door was nearly impossible with the wailing woman and the digital screech of the computer alarms behind him. But he could hear one other sound in the tunnel: the clatter of rocks.

CHAPTER

FIVE

Harry slipped around the corner of the doorway, and stepped into the tunnel, careful to keep low and out of sight. A rock the size of a soccer ball skipped across the worn floor of the tunnel and rolled to a stop within twenty feet of him.

His breath quickened in his chest as he raised the shotgun and peered into the darkness beyond the purple hue of the UV fence. He couldn't see anything. Or anyone.

Another rock, smaller this time, about the size of a baseball streaked past his head and smashed into the bracing around the main entrance. The clanging sound reverberated through the tunnel and brought more bits of rock and clouds of dust down in its wake, thick enough to obscure the entrance.

Harry stared up at the tunnel ceiling barely seven feet above his head. The engineering firm he had commissioned had installed a lattice work of metal bracing to fortify the tunnel, but they gave no guarantees. They definitely didn't count on their equipment being attacked by rock wielding maniacs.

The alarm wailed from his computer terminal behind him as he watched the purple light of UV FENCE #2 fade and die.

It's now or never.

After a deep breath, Harry forced himself to inch deeper into the tunnel, into the inky darkness. Even a dozen feet into the tunnel the sounds of the screaming woman and the screeching of the computer alarms were dampened, absorbed by the smothering darkness. The growing quiet filled with the wheeze of Harry's laboured breathing and the scrape of his boots on the stone floor.

Moving fast and keeping low, he found shelter behind a rocky outcropping that sprouted from the tunnel wall and switched off his light. He was close enough to the first UV fence that he didn't need it. The heat baking down from the light array warmed him through his wet clothes.

Only UV FENCE #1 was operating at full capacity, but the array was powerful enough to grow tomatoes. Ten minutes under the lamps and you'd come away as sunburned as if you laid buck naked on a beach in Aruba for a week.

Harry crouched behind the outcropping and slowly lifted his head, trying to spy what lay beyond the reach of UV FENCE #1. Shadows flickered on the rock walls but there was nothing to shoot at. Only darkness. Raising the rifle, he stepped out into the light. A rock sailed out of the darkness and barely missed his head. The rock exploded against the tunnel ceiling and showered him with bits of stone. More rocks and dust rained down threatening to bury him.

Anger flared in Harry's chest as he squeezed the shotgun and took aim at the dark. He was tired of playing defense. He wasn't some weak academic. He had been on safari. He had climbed Everest, for Christ's sake! He had been chased by rebels and had had gunfights over relics with agents of dubious countries around the world. He was no stranger to violence. Sure, those mad days were at least thirty years in the rearview, but still. He was not about to be bullied. His prize was not about to be stolen. Especially not now. Not when he was so close.

Harry waited until he heard the shuffle-scrape of feet on the stone floor and then stepped out from cover. Another rock, basketball sized, arced out of the darkness and struck the portable transformer that supplied power to UV FENCE #1. The metal box that was bolted to the floor took the brunt of the hit. The UV lights flickered but remained on. Harry saw that the silver metal housing was caved in on the right side and it now leaned off center, but the power still flowed.

It was decision time. If the power to the final fence failed he would be left in the dark with only the weak beam of the light attached to his rifle. He had to stop their advance now.

Right now.

Behind him the woman in the bunker began to

scream again. Her voice was hoarse and cracked from the continuous use, but she would not stop.

How could someone scream for that long?

Again a pineapple sized boulder buzzed the power transformer, but missed. Harry couldn't wait any more. He rose from behind his shelter and raised his shotgun aiming the barrel down the tunnel at a shape standing just beyond the reach of the UV lights.

The shape was of a man, but it couldn't be. The top of the man's head nearly grazed the roof of the tunnel.

Harry aimed the beam of purple light at the man's chest and found not pale skin, but a dark textured hide. The man's body was covered in something. Mud or blood or both. The man stood there defiant and didn't flinch.

Holy shit...

A sound cut through the tunnel. Clicking and hissing. A sound he recognized. It was the same language spoken by the woman. It was not a language that would or could be used to describe love, or empathy. It sounded as beautiful as stereo instructions. Hard consonants and vowels that slid together in a slurry of sounds.

The giant in the tunnel barked his reply and shifted to his right as another figure, this one smaller, raced up to his side and hurled a baseball sized stone at Harry. The projectile burned through the dark so fast he had no time to react.

All Harry could do was scream, *"Don't!"*

One second the stone was in the figure's hand and the next it struck Harry on the thigh. Harry heard a crack and a white hot bolt of pain shot through his body and sent him to the rock floor screaming in agony. He couldn't breathe. He couldn't walk. His leg dragged behind him, twisted and useless and he could feel blood soaking into his pant leg.

Harry clawed his way to his fallen shotgun and pulled himself into a sitting position. Rocks exploded all around him showering him with bits of stone and shrouding the tunnel in a veil of dust. The tunnel itself quaked and trembled as more and more boulders slammed into its fragile walls and weakening supports.

The UV lights of fence #1 flickered, waned and finally died, dropping the tunnel into darkness. Harry twisted on the stone floor of the tunnel and spied the weak white light of the bunker, a mile away.

Using the outcropping and gripping the timbers of the tunnel, Harry pulled himself, gasping to his feet, and aimed his shotgun back toward the darkness and the scratching of nails on stone.

He fired blindly into the shadows and for a second the muzzle flash illuminated a mob of dark figures creeping ever closer. The blast must have hit someone because a wail of bright pain exploded from the dark.

Harry racked the shotgun and fired again as he hopped backward toward the bunker.

"Stay back!" Harry roared, firing a third time into the swirling clouds of dust behind him. The mountain rumbled dangerously and Harry knew he must have hit one of the support beams. He quickened his pace toward the bunker and toward the screech of the wailing woman, rattling the metal walls of her cage as if she were attempting to pull the thing apart.

A moment later Harry's own voice roared out of the dark. Harry stopped. It wasn't an echo. It was his voice. A near perfect replica.

"Stay back!" The voice shouted in perfect Harry speak.

"Stay back!"

The words were exact, but the inflection was off. As if the words were recited by a computer who had never heard the English language.

Do they understand?

A shadow detached itself from the dark and exploded out of the hazy gloom. Arms pumping, legs churning, and with a mouth full a ragged teeth it came barreling straight for Harry.

CHAPTER

SIX

H arry wasted no time. He raised the rifle and
pulled the trigger in one smooth motion and
the shotgun roared in the confined space. For
a split second the muzzle flash illuminated a human
figure, coated in black mud, leaves and lichen, arms
outstretched, talon tipped fingers reaching for him.

The shotgun blast hit the figure in the throat nearly
decapitating the wretched creature in a spray of arterial
blood before the body was thrown violently backward
and darkness smothered the brief burst of light. Harry's
ears rung but he was still able to hear the figure's flesh
crash to the rock floor with a wet slap.

But the figure wasn't dead.

There was no silence.

Harry swept the thin UV light attached to the end of
his rifle toward the floor and found the creature he shot
twisting and writhing on the blood splattered ground.

Its hands were wrapped around its ruined throat as

blood pumped in thick jets through its dirty fingers. He saw that the coating on their skin was some sort of homemade camouflage, crafted from mud, and some of it had been washed away or dried and simply fallen off.

Harry played the UV light over the creature's skin beneath, the color of whole milk, and watched with sick fascination as the thing's flesh burned and peeled from its bones like birch bark in a bonfire.

The creature's anguished cries faded to a low gurgle and finally the thing grew still.

A deep roar erupted further along the tunnel as another rock sailed past Harry's head so close he could feel the breeze from the passing projectile. Harry whirled toward the approaching threat and fired into the dark. In the muzzle flash he couldn't see anyone but the tunnel shuddered again. More rocks and dust spilled out of the ceiling as the mountain itself seemed to grumble in pain.

Harry pulled himself to his feet and half hopped and half limped back toward the door to the bunker. The fight was over. He needed to retreat. The mountain continued to shake, grinding down the supports he had placed inside the crumbling tunnel. In the dark he could hear the metal shriek as it bent under the weight, the older timbers snapping like kindling. Boulders the size of suitcases began to wriggle out of the ceiling with the vibrations and crash to the floor.

Quick footsteps scraping over stone spiked a shot of adrenaline through his veins and forced him to spin, raising the shotgun. Without aiming or even seeing the invisible threat, Harry fired. The gun thundered in the growing din of shifting rock. He didn't wait to see what he hit, if anything. He turned and quickened his awkward hobble to the door and the safety of the bunker beyond.

Harry tried to count how many shots he'd used already and his mind wouldn't cooperate. Was it three? Five? Was he out of shells? His gnarled hand dug into the pocket of his parka. When he withdrew his hand shells spilled to the floor, rolling away in the dark leaving him with only two. His blood soaked hands were shaking so badly he could barely push the shell through the loading port.

The thunder of metric tons of rock shifting toward him drowned out all other sound and thought. Boulders the size of compact cars slammed into the tunnel floor behind him quickly sealing off the shaft as clouds of dust and bits of rock swirled in the dark. The roar of the mountain grew apocalyptic, as if the dark gods within have finally awakened after eons of slumber to destroy the world.

Harry gripped the loaded rifle with both hands as he pushed himself forward dragging his lame leg behind like a stubborn anchor. Step, drag, step, drag and after every step the once bright white doorway grows dim and then dimmer still, the light veiled by a gauzy curtain of dust and debris.

He can feel the door. The smooth cold metal, comfortably an inch and a half thick with two sliding bolts. He was wrong to stay here. He was stupid and stubborn to think he could warn these things off. He knew why they were here. He knew why they would come. They were here for the woman. They were here for their family.

Something bellowed in pain behind him. A mournful cry born of either physical or emotional pain, but pain nonetheless. Harry forced himself not to turn, not even to slow his pace. The door was so close. The air was brightening. He could see the disappointed face of the woman, glaring at him through the bars. She rattled the bars of her cage and screamed once again competing with the voice of the mountain, hot tears spilling over her grimy cheeks, splattering on the stone floor.

Ten feet away from the door a rock the size of a Halloween pumpkin dropped soundlessly from the ceiling and struck Harry in the right shoulder. The bones that made up the cradle of that particular joint cracked and splintered as easily as dry kindling. Harry opened his mouth to scream but all the air had been sucked out of his lungs by the intense pain. He collapsed to the floor, facedown. In the gloom he could see the open doorway and the outline of his shotgun lying uselessly, a few feet away.

Uncaring, the mountain continued to protest and shift and move, dropping more huge stones into the tunnel that exploded on contact sending razored shards in all directions. Crawling madly on his belly, leaving a wide smear of blood in his wake, Harry crawled forward using his good arm and his good leg with little effect. Harry finally found his voice and screamed as the white hot pain of another stone, this one the size of a suitcase, landed on his lower back and crushed his pelvis into unrecognizable shards. Blood filled Harry's mouth, but still his eyes were fixed on the doorway. Desperately close and impossibly far away.

An animal roared somewhere in the shadows and with his good hand Harry reached for the light, before, with one final monstrous grunt, the mountain settled into place, barricading the doorway, and sealing what remained of the tunnel in darkness.

CHAPTER

SEVEN

"Can you turn up the wipers?"

Nick Jackson gripped the fake leather steering wheel hard enough to make the plastic creak. He forced himself to keep his eyes on the road and made a conscious effort, that was no small feat, to not cut a withering glance at his wife sitting in the passenger seat.

The snow was getting heavier and he had *thought* of adjusting the wipers, but she wasn't driving. What did she care? As long as he could see.

Nick and Julie Jackson had been married for seventeen years, dating for three before that and most of their time together could be described as good, if not great, at times. The last two years excluded.

Julie's fringe of blonde hair covered her face as she gave up on trying to peer out through the streaked and snow covered windshield of their ancient Dodge Caravan and turned her attention back to one of her interior

33

design magazines; *Home Decor* or *This Old House* or some such shit. Everything looked the same to Nick. Barn board kitchen. Barn board bathroom. Everything was barn board these days. An accent that was supposed to look worn and rustic, but actually cost an arm and a leg.

He reached for the wiper controls and flicked up the speed a notch. The nearly bald, all season tires of the van skidded through a thick pile of dirty slush and he felt the whole van slide to the right. His stomach did a quick forward roll before he regained control.

He cut his eyes to the right but Julie hadn't looked up.

Maybe she didn't feel it?

"And can you slow down a bit?" Julie said, turning the page of her magazine.

"Do you want to drive?" He snapped, and instantly regretted it. The words came out of his mouth like a whip and he could tell by the way his wife's jaw clenched tight he just landed himself in a fight.

This morning he woke up angry.

Nick had been doing that a lot lately and he didn't know why. Of course, there was a million little reasons, but lately he walked around with a hair trigger that at the same time frightened him and exhausted him.

Someone counting out change at the store in front of him took too long and Nick could feel himself boiling inside. His son chewed with his mouth open at the dinner table made him furious and even though he wouldn't say anything, his glaring, disgusted look was enough to catch the ire of wife.

She had gently suggested he go to therapy, and he declined. Not only because his heath benefits no longer covered it after he was laid off, but it was an easy excuse.

A simple look, one from his *'I'm so annoyed'* collection and she wouldn't talk to him for days before she cornered him and lectured him about how the kids were frightened around him. About how they felt like they couldn't do or say anything around him for fear of getting him upset. Of course then he would go on the defense and really get the argument going. Throwing all the gas he had on the fire hoping to burn them both to the ground.

Was that what he wanted?

Was he done? With marriage, kids, everything?

He knew he was exhausted from going to job interviews at forty-six. He knew that. He knew he was feeling shitty about the apartment. It seemed the only time he and Julie spoke was either about the kids or how he was always grumpy. They hadn't had sex since his birthday and that was in March, here it was December and three days before Christmas.

A corner of the magazine curled down and Julie stared at him over the edge.

"Do you want me to drive?" She asked. "Are you tired?"

She was giving him an out, and he knew it. An olive branch. It was his to take.

Nick gripped the wheel again, let his foot off the gas a few degrees and focused on his breathing. He had promised. Not only to Julie, but to himself, that he would not fuck this weekend up. He would not be moody and poison the well, as Julie put it, with his negativity and veiled hostility. With phrases like that Nick wondered sometimes whether she was going to therapy without him. She had stopped mentioning it to him, begging him really, to go. Maybe they should go? Maybe it would help? Not that they had the money for things like that any more.

Nick's eyes flicked to the gas gauge. Just below half. Then his mind ran to their bank account, perpetually slipping into overdraft more and more each week. They barely had enough money for this stupid trip.

He felt the old rage swell in his chest just thinking about their destination and what awaited them: Richie Mellon, Julie's brother.

He owned Mellon Markets, those weird stores where it was half fresh market and half diner. He started the first one straight out of college and now he had over a hundred locations. After Nick had lost his job at the mill Richie had hinted that he was looking to step aside a little bit, enjoy the good life while he was still young and still had lead in the pencil.

He had hinted at Nick taking over a vacancy as regional manager; taking some of the day to day off of Richie's plate. The thought of working for his brother-in-law, of reporting to him on a daily basis made Nick want to chew broken glass. But, for the last three months he had sent his resume to every company in a fifty mile radius. No one was hiring, and definitely no one was hiring a forty-six year old former regional manager at the salary and benefits package he was used to. That was for sure.

"Hun?" Julie asked again, her tone light although Nick still noticed the muscles in her jaw were bunched. She was trying so hard. "I can drive if you want?"

"No." He said evenly, and then a little softer. "Sorry."

He could feel her eyes on him, lingering, waiting for something more. He could never tell which direction she wanted to go in these days. Did she want him to fight more? Apologize more? He kept his hands on the wheel and his eyes on the road.

"I'm just..." Nick started and then shook his head, and made an effort to brighten his voice. "You hungry?"

EIGHT

J ulie closed her magazine and laid it across her lap and swivelled to inspect their children.

Oscar, '*Ozzy*', was thirteen and with his thick black hair and skinny frame he was the very double of Nick in his youth. Awkward and shy, and introverted to the point of near catatonia, he would dive into his digital books stored on his tablet and read for days, without eating if Julie let him.

He sat slouched against a pillow wedged against the passenger door, his face obscured by his tablet. His sister, Tara, sixteen going on thirty sat scrolling through social media, her ear buds permanently peeking out behind the lazy curls of her long blonde hair.

"Hey, you guys hungry?" Julie said.

The kids ignored her as usual.

"Ozzy, honey." Julie said as she grabbed his knee. "You hungry?"

Ozzy's head snapped up for a second as he thought

about the alien prospect of food and shrugged, his bright blue eyes never leaving the tablet.

"Did you know that this area has more wolves per square mile than people?" He said.

"I didn't know that." Julie replied. "It's kinda scary."

"It's not scary, mom." He said. "Wolves are way more scared of us."

"Well, that's good."

Julie had to turn nearly all the way around in her seat to reach Tara and when she did, the contact with her older daughter's leg shocked the teenager as if she were poked with an electric cattle prod.

"Jesus!" Tara snapped, sitting bolt upright in her seat and pulling the earbuds from her ears.

"Language." Julie said.

"What are you doing? What's going on?"

Tara pulled out her earbuds and winced staring out through the snowfields outside her window as if she just woke up here and hadn't been driving for the last five hours with her family.

"Where are we?" She asked.

"What's going on is we are gonna stop for some food. Are you hungry?" Julie asked her.

"Eat where?" She asked, again staring into the forest whipping by on both sides of the highway. Nothing but blowing snow and pine trees and clouds the color of fresh bruises squeezing out the daylight above.

"I saw signs for a diner coming up." Nick told her, meeting her eyes in the rearview.

"A *diner*?" Tara said. "Did we drive into the '50s?"

"A diner is like a restaurant." Oscar explained.

"I know what a diner is, moron." Tara clapped back, jabbing her grinning brother in the ribs.

"Food it is." Nick told them, and signalled to change lanes.

"You know it's not too late to turn back, you know." Tara said to no one in particular.

Again Nick met her eyes and then quickly looked away.

"It was too late two hours ago, honey." Nick told her.

"We could tell them, like, the car broke down." Tara explained.

"Richie would actually believe that." Julie added with a smile.

"There's nothing wrong with Mystical Blue." Nick said stroking the cracked dashboard lovingly. "It's got us this far."

"Wasn't this supposed to be your car? For college?" Oscar asked Tara, goading his sister. "If you had passed your driving test."

Tara shot her brother a stare that may have taken years off his life.

"I miss the Navigator." Tara said.

"Me too." Julie added.

"I don't miss the payments." Nick said, killing the buzz. "That's for sure."

Ozzy pulled his gaze away from the tablet and switched it off.

"Wait...What are we talking about? Are we not going now?"

"No, honey." Julie told him. "We're still going. Tara is just joking."

"'Cause, I'd be fine with going home." Ozzy told them.

Julie spun in her seat.

"I thought you liked your cousins?"

"Carter and Benson?" Ozzy said. "They're dicks."

"Like father like son." Nick said loud enough for only Julie to hear. It was a stupid move, but he did it anyways and Julie cut him a sharp glance.

"Come on. Really?"

Nick shrugged.

"He is, Mom." Tara agreed. "Last year at Thanksgiving Uncle Richie told me that I'd be prettier if I was taller."

"What the hell does that even mean?" Nick asked. "You're beautiful honey."

"Thanks, Dad."

"That's just creepy." Ozzy added.

"Okay." Julie said, a little louder than she needed to. "Look, your Uncle Richie can be--"

"A real ass?" Tara finished for her.

"Difficult, Tara. At times." Julie said, giving her the look that meant playtime was over and she was really serious. "And if I'm being honest, a bit of a jerk, but he's planned this big family holiday--"

"--and he's paying." Ozzy said.

Julie let her eyes slide closed to give her strength to continue and said to everyone, "So, we're going, okay...and it's gonna be great. Right?"

Julie waited for the two kids to meet her gaze and nod their agreement.

"*Right?*" She repeated.

And when they finally nodded to each other, then to their Mom Julie spun back in her seat and snatched up her magazine.

A few moments of silence as long haul truckers passed on the left, the turbulence from their passing enough to push the mini van toward the opposite shoulder across the ice, forcing Nick to compensate.

For a while no one spoke. The only sound in the van was from the Sam Cooke Greatest Hits CD leaking through the tinny speakers and the thrum of the van's wheels on the highway. Until...

"So, why are we doing Christmas all the way up here instead of at his *casa*, like always?" Nick asked.

"You can't ski in Seattle, Nick." Julie told him flipping through her magazine aimlessly. "Besides, Chantal told me they were having the floors in the great room redone."

A longer silence as Julie studied an article on revitalizing your garden shed.

"Great room, huh?" Nick said, smiling at Julie, caressing her thigh. "We have one of those don't we, honey?"

"We used to." Julie replied cooly.

Whatever remained of Nick's good mood felt like it just got its neck broken and was left to die. He removed his hand from his wife's leg and replaced it on the steering wheel.

"Did you know these mountains have one of the longest tunnel systems in the world." Ozzy announced. "The article I read said that there may be hundreds of miles of tunnels and passageways. There was these hikers--"

"Okay, we get it..." Tara said. "You have no friends."

"Tara, be nice to your brother." Julie said. "At least he's learning something. Better than scrolling through Tik Tok and frying your brain on Instagram."

Tara opened her mouth to respond when Ozzy pulled her close so only she could hear him.

"Keep making fun of me and I'll tell Mom and Dad about your tattoo."

Tara's eyes popped wide with surprise as the blood drained from her face.

CHAPTER

NINE

It took another hour for the Jacksons to pull off the highway and into the Dixie Land Truck Stop. Nick found a spot wedged between a newer Ford Explorer and wouldn't you know it, a goddamn Lincoln Navigator. He dropped the Caravan into park and felt the engine shudder, rattling the empty coffee cups in the cup holders, before it finally went quiet. Nick tore his eyes away from his former vehicle and caught Julie staring at it as well.

"Christ." Tara said. "I'm gonna explode."

"Stop saying that." Julie said. "Stop taking the Lord's name in vain."

"Okay, Jes— *geez.*" Tara said. "I just really gotta pee."

"Keep an eye on your brother." Nick told her. "Stay together."

"Tara," Julie said. "Wait."

The girl did as she was told and Julie handed her two twenties.

"Get burgers for everybody." She told her. "We'll be right in."

"Everything okay?"

"Everything's fine." She said, adding a smile to sell it. "Go on. We'll be right in."

Both kids unclipped their belts and stepped out into the blowing snow, careful to hold the handle of their car doors to prevent them from getting caught by the wind and getting whipped into the vehicles parked along side.

When both car doors slammed shut it was just Julie and Nick alone in the van. With the engine off, Nick could immediately feel the temperature drop. Snow piled on the windshield, obscuring their view of their two children jogging through the storm and jumping the piles of dirty slush to the front doors of the truck stop diner.

"I'm sorry if I was short with you." Nick said. "Earlier."

Julie didn't look at him. She kept staring out into the snow. She nodded though, so he knew she was listening.

"I know you didn't want to go." Julie said. "To come here."

"Does anyone?" Nick said, sparking Julie to spin in her seat to stare at him. "I'm serious, the kids don't even want to go and —"

"We need this, Nick." Julie said. "Not only is it a vacation, a break from...*everything*. Richie could really help us."

Nick couldn't help it. The rage, the frustration, the worry that kept him up at night. The feeling of being

45

helpless. Helpless to help his family. To provide. He shook his head, looking away.

"I'm still waiting to hear back from Barry over at Maple Farms." He told her.

"It's been three weeks."

"Corporate decisions take time." He countered. "Look I don't know what's going on over there, let's just wait and see before we make any rash decisions."

"Nick, we already lost the house and the car." Julie said.

"We didn't *lose* the house and the car." He said. "We sold them."

"Because we couldn't afford them."

"Still."

"I'm working as much as I can." She said. "But we're still falling behind. A job with Richie doesn't have to be the end. It doesn't have to be forever."

"It feels like it. It feels like I'm making a deal with the devil."

"It doesn't have to be." Julie told him. "Think of it as a life line. A second chance."

He saw it then. He saw it in her eyes. She was hoping he wouldn't fuck this up. He wouldn't drink too much and say something that he would regret: something cutting about Richie's spoiled kids, or his sheltered wife. Or just sit and sulk like he did last Christmas. He was fighting city hall and losing. *Badly.*

"I know you're trying, honey." She whispered. "I know you are and I know how frustrated you are. And I know you don't want to do this. I get it. This is the last

46

thing you want to do, but sometimes the only choice is the least shitty one."

Nick chuckled, slipping his hand over her thigh again. This time, she covered his hand with her own and raised him a squeeze.

"The shittiest." He said.

"Totally."

She smiled at him then. It had been a long time since she smiled at him and it felt like the sun had broken through the clouds, if only for a moment. She held his face in her hands and kissed him softly on the lips. It was a small kiss, but it was enough. For a moment he had what he wanted.

"Come on." She said, pulling away. "The kids'll think we left without them."

CHAPTER

TEN

I nside the diner Tara flushed the toilet using her shoe and turned sideways as she left the bathroom stall hoping to avoid touching anything in this place. The sink was going to be nasty. She always found that women were cleaner than men, but in this place the women were giving the men a run for their money.

Wads of wet paper towel were left on the floor and all over the bathroom counter top. The sink was coated with flecks of black hair, both long and short and even some curlies. It made Tara want to gag.

She pulled a fresh paper towel from the dispenser, and used it to cover her palm as she twisted on the tap. A choked gurgle issued from somewhere within the plumbing before rust coloured water leaked from the faucet. Again she used the paper towel to squirt some pink soap into her palm and washed up as best she could with what she could only assume was well water.

Feeling somehow dirtier after she washed her hands

A DARK BREED

she stepped into the narrow hallway and made her way back to the diner and her table, when something pinned to a corkboard made her stop.

The message board was plastered with announcements covering everything from lost dogs to guitar lessons to used furniture, but what caught her eye was the missing posters.

A quick count in her head and she saw that there was thirteen. Some of them were older, dating back ten, fifteen years, but some of them were newer. Old, young, and somewhere in the middle, the smiling faces of the missing stared out from the curled yellowed notices.

"'Scuse me, sweetheart."

Tara turned to find the owner of the gravelly voice was a woman in her fifties, decked out in denim from head to toe. A belt buckle the size of a dinner plate held back a belly pressing the buttons of her denim shirt into surrender. Her gray blonde hair was pulled tight into a long braided ponytail that slipped over her shoulder and nearly made it to her waist.

"Sorry." Tara mumbled and pressed herself to the far wall allowing the older woman to pass.

"Shame." The woman said, nodding toward the sad billboard.

"Why are there so many?" Tara asked. The woman stopped and thought for a second, pondering the question, her head tilted to one side.

"Well, honey, I don't rightly know." The woman said after a time. "But if I had to guess, I would blame it on city folks watching too many episodes of the nature channel and then coming out here thinking they were Daniel Boone."

"Who's Daniel Boone?"

The woman smiled wryly.

"Goddamn I'm old." She said. "Ask your dad. And just get to where you're going and stay outta them woods, you hear?"

Tara nodded and the woman smiled back. "Good girl."

Tara wandered into the warm diner, her stomach grumbling with the smell of french fries and grease and realized just how hungry she was. She found Ozzy in a booth by the window, munching on a fry, the rest of the family's food arranged in front of their places, but he was the only one there. Tara slid into the booth opposite her brother and popped one of his fries into her mouth.

"Where's the parental units?"

Ozzy tossed a curl of his dark hair out of his eyes and gestured with his chin toward the parking lot. Tara saw her mother's slight frame pacing back and forth in the snow, the curl of cigarette smoke mixed with her own warm breath rising from her head.

"I thought she quit?" Tara said.

Ozzy shrugged and plucked another fry out of the box. They had both listened to their mother swear up and down on too many occasions that she was going to quit for good this time. And this time she meant it. She loved them too much to develop throat cancer or mouth cancer, and leave them orphaned.

And then the monthly bills would roll in or the car would break down or a pipe would burst and she would head to the kitchen, and pull her cigarettes out of the freezer where she kept them hidden in a ziplock bag.

Tara wondered what brought on the cigarettes today. It was supposed to be a happy day. Christmas in the mountains in a luxurious chalet, all paid for by their wealthy, if not creepy, Uncle Rich.

"You think they'll get divorced?" Ozzy asked.

"What?" Tara said quickly, maybe a little too quickly. "No."

"Why not?"

Tara stared at her little brother searching his blue eyes. He really did want a reason. He wanted her to convince him. With evidence and examples of their parents overflowing love for one another. But she had nothing. They fought, like everybody fought on occasion, but they never really seemed happy. At night they would sit together watching their shows, but they sat on opposite ends of the couch or in different chairs. They never sat together any more.

"I don't know, buddy." She said finally. "I think they want to stay together. They want to make it work."

"I hear mom crying sometimes. At night." Ozzy said, tears of his own pooling in his eyes.

Tara wasn't the emotional one. She didn't cry at movies or get overcome with anything, but she could see

PATRICK MCNULTY

how hurt her brother was. How much he needed something. Anything to hold onto.

She reached for him and gripped his hand, and for a moment she thought he might pull away, but he left it where it was on the scarred table top.

"If they need money..." he said, "I can give them mine...I have some from birthdays and stuff."

Tara smiled at him and squeezed his hand.

"Dad got laid off." Tara said. "Half the town did when the mill closed. They sold the house cause they knew times would be tough. They stayed ahead of a lot of my friends. Remember Laura Murphy?"

Ozzy nodded, he knew Laura's little brother, Paul. He would always get in trouble in class for drawing homemade tattoos on his arms in ink.

"They had to move to Minnesota." She told him. "So it could be worse."

"Will we have to move?"

Tara shook her head and let Oscar's hand go with a final short squeeze. He still didn't take it off the table top.

"Dad'll get another job, then Mom won't have to work so much. It'll get better. And you can keep your paper route money."

ELEVEN

F our minutes, according to Nick's watch, was all the time it took to bleed the heat from the van. Already frost had formed on the windshield and driver's side window, obscuring his view of the parking lot and the diner beyond inch by inch.

Nick's slow breath formed clouds in the quiet, darkening space. He pulled his phone from his coat pocket and checked his email. He had become obsessive about this task since sending out his resumes over the last three months.

At first he would check it every couple hours, telling himself to relax, to calm down. It took time for prospective companies to sift through the reams of digital flotsam in order to get to his glowing offer. And then that time passed, replaced by a panic that came with the sudden realization that perhaps he too had become part of the flotsam. Part of the debris that had to be shifted aside in order to reach the really valuable offers.

He hadn't sent out resumes since graduating college and now in a world where everyone was looking for the younger, cheaper solution, had he become obsolete?

He was checking for that little red dot on the top right corner of the mail icon every chance he got now. Then even when he didn't see the dot, he tapped the icon anyways, hoping to somehow jog the mail system into action. Forcing the app to go forth and retrieve the email he so desperately wanted to read.

Sitting there in the rapidly cooling van he checked the mail icon again. He even checked the junk mail but there was nothing there except a few emails offering to increase the size of his penis.

He cursed and spied Julie pacing under the awning of the diner, a stream of cigarette smoke trailing behind her as she wore a path through the falling snow. They had made a deal, he and Julie. They would give Barry Wilson, the district manager of Maple Farms until this weekend to make him an offer, if not, Nick had agreed, under duress, to accept her brother Richie's offer of employment.

Nick had argued with Julie to give Barry more time, he had only been interviewed three weeks ago and with the holiday season coming up and everyone putting work related matters on the back burner, it was normal not to hear anything. Julie didn't agree.

She was tired of waiting. Even with her pulling double shifts at the hospital, the bank and their colorful assortment of creditors were circling like vultures, waiting for them to finally slip up and miss a payment and seize on any excuse to swoop in and take the little they had left.

Nick checked the time on his phone. It was nearly four on a Friday. Last day of business before the new year. Barry would probably be gone for the day.

What was he so worried about? The interview had gone well. He was definitely qualified. He was just checking in. Following up. Nothing wrong with that Julie told him. It shows you're interested.

It screams you're desperate, Nick thought.

He took another look at his wife, her arms wrapped around her thin frame, hunched against the cold. She had begun to look tired even after a solid night's sleep. The bags beneath her eyes claiming permanent residence.

Nick scrolled through the contacts in his phone and tapped on Barry Wilson.

A female voice answered on the third ring announcing that he had reached Barry Wilson's office. Nick announced himself and to his surprise she connected him right away.

"Almost missed me, Nick." Barry said. "Just getting ready to head home."

Barry's voice was faraway and Nick could tell he had been put on speaker phone.

"I appreciate you taking the call, Barry."

"No problem." Barry said. "No problem at all. What can I do for you?"

"Well, I was just heading up north for the holidays."

"Oh yeah? Where abouts?"

"My brother-in-law rented some chalet on Whistler's Peak."

"Oh wow, fla-dee-dah."

"Yeah, thanks. I don't want to keep you but—"

"Nick, we haven't made any decisions yet." Barry told him. "Like I told you before, the board meets again after the holidays but as soon as I know, I will let you know. I promise."

"I appreciate that, Barry." Nick said. "You know how it is."

"I do, Nick. I do."

Nick doubted he knew at all what he was talking about. He knew Barry Wilson from college. Barry had drunk, snorted and fucked his way through four years without a care in the world, confident in the fact that whatever the outcome he had a cushy corner office waiting for him in the end in the family business.

He never had to worry about missing a bill payment or a wife working herself to the bone in a hospital where gunshot wounds were more common than heart attacks. He didn't have to worry about selling his house for less than market value in order to escape claiming bankruptcy.

He definitely didn't know what it was like driving in a rusted out piece of shit Dodge Caravan that leaked oil like a sieve and was barely held together with duct tape.

He didn't have a fucking clue.

"Dad said he wanted to revisit all new hires again in the new year." Barry finished. "Make his decision with a clear head."

Nick groaned into the phone before he could catch himself and quickly prayed that Barry didn't hear it, but it was too late.

"I know. I know." Barry said. "Dad can be a little difficult, but he won't be around forever, as he always tells us."

"I hear you, Barry."

"Hang in there, Nick. I can tell you that you're my pick. I just don't get the final say."

"Thanks again, Barry."

"Okay, have fun on those mountains okay? But not too much fun. I'll talk to you in the new year. We'll set something up."

Nick heard the sound of ice swirling in a crystal highball glass and then the call disconnected.

He stared at the phone balanced on the dashboard as the call light disappeared and the glass surface went black.

Fuck.

He snatched up the phone and stuffed it in his pocket, wrenched open the door and stepped into the blowing snow. Thick flakes weren't spiralling poetically anymore. The romance and beauty of the snow storm was gone. Curtains of white swept past the little diner and all but obliterated the red neon OPEN signs as they passed.

Nick tucked his head into the collar of his coat and made a bee-line to the front entrance.

CHAPTER

TWELVE

J ulie lit her second cigarette and took an epic haul pulling the nicotine deep into her lungs. She held it for a second before letting it slowly out through her nostrils. The temperature was dropping and the icy wind cut through her jeans like they weren't there. She finished the last of her cigarette in two quick pulls and enjoyed the way the nicotine blast made her feel light headed. It made what she was about to do a little easier.

She pitched the butt into a mound of dirty snow beside the entrance to the little diner and dug her cell phone out of her pocket. Her fingers were freezing and shaking a little from the cold and the nicotine coursing through her veins, but she managed to open her contacts and tap MOM.

She pressed the phone to her ear and prayed no one picked up.

Please let it go to voicemail.

But she knew it wouldn't happen. They were three hours late and her mother always had her cell on her. The woman usually answered the phone so fast it was as if she kept the device in a holster on her hip like some old timey gunslinger. Julie smiled at the image of her seventy-three year old mother wearing assless chaps.

"Oh my god." Her mother said without preamble. "Richie and I were worried sick."

I'll bet. Julie thought.

"Are you all right? Are the kids all right? Say something."

"Mom." Julie said, as calm as she could muster. "We're fine."

A gust of wind carrying a wall of snow swept beneath the awning where she stood and she took the full force of the blast straight in the face. Julie spun away a moment too late and swore.

"Julie, what happened?" Her mother crowed from the phone. "Why are you swearing?"

Julie swore again under her breath and did her best to wipe the cell phone down.

"I'm outside." She told her mother.

"Why are you outside?" And then to someone else, "Their car broke down. Julie is outside. On the side of the road."

"No." Julie said. "Mom, we're fine."

"Where did your car break down?" Her mother wanted to know.

"No. I...We're on our way." Julie said.

"You're still coming?"

"Yes, Mom."

Another howling gust of wind swept through the lot and she saw Nick, head down, make his way through the lot. When he saw her she held up a finger. He didn't look happy, and Julie's heart sank a little.

He mouthed, *You okay?*

She nodded and then she watched him head inside. Julie heard a rustling sound as the phone switched hands and then her younger brother Richie came on the line.

"The hell is going on?" He said, and Julie could hear the slight slur in his words that made everything he said kind of slide together.

"Mom says you're outside, on the side of the road? What happened?"

She could picture him now standing in his rented chalet that was bigger than most people's homes. Two hundred dollar haircut, a new Rolex. It was as if he looked up rich douche bag in the dictionary and then made that his life goal. Added to that he sounded like he was on his third scotch of the afternoon.

"Where are you?" He said between sips. "Send me a pin, I'll come get you. Told mom you shoulda kept the Navigator. Don't know what you're thinking driving up here in the mountains in that piece of shit."

"*Richie.*" Julie heard her mom scold her brother. "*Language.*"

"Sorry, Ma. But seriously. That's my niece and

60

nephew he's got in that piece of crap. It's not safe. Not up in the mountains. And it's *snowing*."

Julie heard his mother say something but it was muffled and quick, and not meant for her to hear and then Richie said, "Still, in this economy we all gotta tighten our belts but not cheap out on safety."

The two of them together were insufferable.

Sometime during the weekend her mother would inevitably corner her in the kitchen or somewhere private and ask her if she needed money, or if she and the kids needed to stay with her and dad for a while. Excluding Nick in the invitation as if losing your job was somehow a contagious disease.

And Richie would tell her not to worry, because he would float her for a while. A gift. A loan if it made her feel better.

She would rather eat rat poison.

And to think that she had pleaded with Nick to take Richie's job offer, to get something, so that maybe she didn't have to work every available overtime shift to make ends meet. Now, she didn't know what to think. How could Nick work for her brother? How could anyone?

Julie wanted to strangle her little brother, right through the phone if she could. Squeeze his perfectly coiffed head until it popped.

"Okay, Rich, you're cutting out." Julie lied. "Reception up here is the worst. Be there soon."

"Wait, where are you?" Richie asked. "I'll come and get you. The roads up here are something else."

"Okay, bye."

Julie killed the call and then screamed through clenched teeth into the wintery void. When she opened her eyes she saw a chubby truck driver in a John Deere cap had stopped walking toward the diner, waiting to see what happened next with the crazy lady blocking the entrance.

She gave the man a smile and a little wave before her phone rang again.

Richie.

She declined the call, set her phone to silent and slipped through the double doors into the warmth and light of the diner.

JULIE PULLED open the door to the diner and the warmth and smells of fried food washed over her, instantly melting the crusts of snow that had formed on her eyebrows and in her hair. She unzipped her parka and spotted her family hunched over their food in a booth near the back.

She hung her parka on a hook and took a seat next to Nick. She slid a hand over his thigh and gave him a quick peck on his warm, stubbly cheek.

"What's that for?"

"I'm gonna need you as an alibi when I murder my brother." She told him.

Ozzy and Tara chuckled, toying with the last of the fries on their plates.

"How bad was it?" Nick asked.

Julie bit into her lukewarm cheeseburger and immediately felt better. She answered around a mouthful of meat and cheese.

"On a scale of one to douche? Douche." She told him. "He thought the Caravan broke down, it was as if they were expecting it. He said he would come and get us."

Nick checked his watch. "Yeah, right. It's after four, he's probably lit by now."

"Oh he is, but he would still come." Julie said chomping on her fries. "Richie the hero."

"Then let's just go home." Tara said. "We could say the van did break down and...there's gotta be a hotel near by. We could stay over and then make like this never happened."

"Yeah. Seriously." Ozzy added. "Or we could go to Florida. Anywhere."

Julie took a sip of her Coke and asked Nick, "How 'bout you? How'd your call go?"

"They aren't gonna make any decisions until after the holidays."

"Could he give you anything?" She asked. "A hint?"

Nick shook his head.

"Barry pretends he's in on the decisions, but really he'll hire whoever his dad tells him to."

Julie took another bite of her burger, nearly finishing the thing in three bites. Nick could see her mind spinning, working out all the calculations. The kids looked to him to nudge the decision to go home over the finish line, but he knew better than to try and bully his wife.

Almost twenty years of marriage trained him to

attack every negotiation with the patience of the ninja. He could tell she was torn right now, right on the fence. She could fall either way, but it had to be her decision.

Nick settled into the booth and munched on a fry, and waited.

"Mom, come on, Uncle Richie is a complete tool bag." Tara said.

But Julie was already shaking her head.

"We have to go. We have to."

The kids who had been hunched over the table flopped back against the booth, defeated.

"Grandma and Grandpa are there. They came all the way from Palm Springs and they haven't seen you guys for years. Besides, it's the holidays."

"But you guys hate spending time with your brother." Tara said.

"It's not about that." Julie told them. "You guys will have fun. I'm sure there's gonna be skiing and tubing. It'll be fun."

The kids looked like the next few days would be anything but detention in a slave labor camp.

"Come on." Julie said, and looked to Nick for help. "Right? Try to be happy, okay. This is important. It's family."

"Come on, guys." Nick said, and then to Julie. "At least with your brother there, there's gonna be booze."

Julie and Nick smiled and clinked their plastic cups of soda in a cheers as the tension bled out of the booth.

They stared at each other for a beat longer than necessary, holding that grin. Sharing that secret knowledge that, at the very least, they were on the same side. And they had each other's back.

In that moment, in that cracked leatherette booth, with the warmth of his wife's thigh pressing against his, Nick Jackson was the happiest he would ever be.

THIRTEEN

With their feet warm and their bellies full, the Jacksons stood bundled up against the cold between the double doors of the diner. The Jacksons could barely see their van through the storm as the howling wind hurled sheets of snow armored with nails of ice at the glass doors.

The Navigator that had been parked beside them had left allowing a drift of snow to accumulate against the driver side of the Caravan as if the blizzard was actively trying to hide their ancient ride.

As the wind whistled through the gaps in the entrance doors Nick was painfully aware that their Caravan did not have the fancy features of their former vehicle. Their old Navigator could be started from anywhere through an app on his phone. He could defrost the windows, heat the interior and even warm the steering wheel.

Nick pulled the key for the Caravan out of his pocket

and saw the red duct tape he had wound around the fob when the plastic molding had cracked and fell away years ago. He couldn't even unlock the doors remotely.

He waited for Ozzy to pull down his toque and then said, "Ready?"

With Nick leading the charge, the Jacksons bent their heads into the wind and hurried through the frozen lot of half buried vehicles to their powder blue van.

Using his glove, Nick dusted the snow away from the driver's side door handle and unlocked the door. He dropped into the driver's seat and unlocked the rest of the doors.

Tara, Ozzy and Julie all found their seats and quickly slammed the doors closed behind them, cutting off the storm and the screech of the wind.

Nick jabbed the key into the ignition and twisted. Lights flickered on the dashboard as the engine whined and coughed and died.

"You gotta be kidding me."

He shot a glance at Julie's pale face.

"I'm not calling my brother." She said. "I would rather freeze to death in this parking lot."

Nick smiled, "Agreed."

"What?" Ozzy said. "What's happening?"

"Nothing buddy." Nick told him and tried the key again. This time the engine caught and roared to life, or as much of a roar as the Caravan could muster.

"Thank God." He whispered.

Immediately icy cold air flowed through the vents as the engine heated up.

Nick pulled the snow brush from the back seat and shouldered open his door to step back out into the storm where he set to cleaning snow from the van's many windows and away from the headlights.

"Mom?" Ozzy said, just above a whisper as Nick stomped around the outside of the van.

Julie swiveled in her seat to face him.

"Are you and Dad getting a divorce?"

Tara looked up from her phone as Julie swiveled in her seat.

"Is that what you're worried about?"

Julie looked from Ozzy to Tara who nodded and suddenly looked a lot younger than her sixteen years.

"We're not getting a divorce, guys. Why would you think that?"

"You just fight all the time and Dad is—"

"Your dad lost his job and that hurt." Julie said. "I know you realize that, but he's trying to get another one, it just takes time. But we both love you very much and we need to stick together. All of us. Okay?"

Julie gripped Ozzy's knee and squeezed forcing a smile out of the boy.

"Okay?" Julie asked Tara. "All of us. Team Jackson, okay? We can get through this. Even with Uncle Ritchie."

Even Tara smiled at that one. Julie could see the start of a tear in Tara's eyes and leaned over the back of the seat to pull her daughter into a hug. Surprisingly, Tara hugged her mother back. Hard.

It felt good and Julie let it linger even as Nick slid back behind the wheel.

Finally Tara released her.

"What's going on? Everything okay?" Nick asked, warming his frozen fingers against the air vents. "I miss something? How come I don't get a hug?"

Promptly Ozzy wrapped his arms around his father's neck from behind and squeezed.

"Thanks buddy."

"Just gathering our strength for the assault on the castle." Julie told him.

"All right guys, we ready?"

"Ready!" Ozzy said, sitting back in his seat and grinning.

"All right, what about you Tear-Bear?" Nick asked.

"Oh my God, don't call me that."

"Then give me an answer."

"I'm ready, Dad."

"Awesome, this is gonna be the best weekend ever." Nick said and felt like he actually meant it.

"Okay, don't overdo it." Julie told him. "How far away are we?"

Nick pulled up the center console and plucked out a folded piece of paper and carefully pressed the map and list of directions flat against the steering wheel.

His fingers traced the line of the highway until the little crossroads.

"Why not just put the address in your phone?" Tara asked him.

"It's just one road, honey and our phones aren't reliable up here. See this is the crossroads where we saw that chocolate factory a while ago." His fingers slid along the paper heading north on the same road. "We need to find the sign for Draper's Creek and then it's Mountain Creek Drive. I'd say we're about an hour away. Maybe two in this weather."

Nick stuffed the map into the centre console and hit the windshield wipers. Already the snow had accumulated on the glass and stayed there, obscuring the window.

"When is it supposed to stop snowing?" Julie asked.

"Up here? I don't know." he said. "June?"

"Hilarious."

"That's why you love me."

"Just drive slow."

"Aye aye captain."

FOURTEEN

A little over two and a half hours later any glow that Nick and Julie shared had begun to fade. As the mountain road twisted higher and higher through the trees the driving conditions worsened along with their moods.

Periodically, the Caravan would shake in the gale force wind as a wall of white would rumble over the vehicle dropping their visibility to zero in every direction.

Nick slowed the van, careful not to stomp on the brakes ever mindful of the guardrail on his right and the barely glimpsed treetops beyond letting him know just how far the drop would be.

The Caravan creaked to a standstill on brakes well past their prime. The wind didn't stop and the view through the windshield didn't clear. They hadn't seen another vehicle in forty minutes and with each mile ticking over on the odometer the road became narrower, the trees on either side of the road drew closer, and the realization became more and more clear that somewhere along the line they had missed their turn.

With the van stopped and the radio long since abandoned, the only sound was the wind squealing through the gaps in the Caravan's defenses, ghostly fingers prying at the spaces between the doors and the chassis. Rattling the windows. Raking its fingers over the hood.

In the backseat the kids were asleep. Ozzy lay against Tara who slept propped up against the rear passenger door. Both kids bundled up against the chill beneath a heavy blue and white blanket emblazoned with the Toronto Maple Leafs logo.

"Try googling the address." Nick said, staring out into the wall of white.

"I tried." Julie replied. "There's still no reception."

Nick leaned a little closer to the windshield, as if that extra few inches would allow him to see through the swirling snow and finally glimpse the exit to Draper's Creek.

"It's gotta be close. I mean. It's one road." Nick said, for the hundredth time.

Julie said nothing. Her right knee jumping a little higher and a little faster than it had an hour earlier. A tic from her days in nursing school that had been making a bit of comeback lately.

A break in the solid wall ahead of them allowed Nick to ease off the brake and let the Caravan roll slowly forward. The first thing he saw was the glint of the guardrail caught in the weak light of their headlights. Julie's breath caught in her throat as they realized how close they were to striking the dented rail. If Julie rolled down her window she could probably reach out and touch it.

She cut her eyes to Nick but he had no response except to crank the steering wheel to the left and aim the rumbling van back toward the center of the road.

"How can there be no service in this day and age?" Nick wanted to know. "Seriously."

Next to him Julie peered at the screen of her cell. No calls or texts went through thanks to the glaring: NO SIGNAL pinned to the top right corner.

She opened the center console and dropped the useless iPhone into the compartment and pulled out the now dog-eared map Nick had printed.

"I didn't see a sign at all on this road." Julie said, running her finger over the map and retracing their steps. "I should've seen a sign. Something."

"It's coming up." Nick told her. "It's got to be."

Julie went back to the map and switched on the overhead light. She found the diner on the map marked with a tiny fork and knife and then used her finger to follow the line of the highway they were on until...

"Oh shit..."

"What?"

Julie shot a glance at the gas gauge before turning to face Nick, but it was too late. He saw her face.

"I don't think we're on the right road."

"What? Of course we are." Nick asked again. "What do you mean?"

Julie angled the map closer to the light and showed Nick a spot on the map where the road they were on split into two.

"This…" Julie said, pointing to the icon of the fork and knife on the map. "…was the diner, that's the highway and this is where we should have turned. See, we should have turned onto Benson's Ridge. See the little fork and knife again. That's the tourist overlook with the cafe. We passed it and Ozzy asked to get ice cream, remember?"

Nick shook his head and switched off the overhead light.

"I can't see shit." He said in response, the old anger firing up again. "And I haven't seen shit since the diner."

"I'm not blaming you." Julie told him.

"That would be a first." Nick said.

"*Nick. Come on.*"

"I can't even see the road." He said.

"What road are we even on?" Julie said, peering out the windshield.

"You're the one with the map, you tell me." He snapped and Julie glared at him.

"Jesus, Nick, calm down, we just need to turn around."

"Where Julie?" He said again, venom in his voice. "Where the fuck are we supposed to turn around? The road is barely wide enough to go forward."

Nick gripped the steering wheel and felt the shame bubble and boil inside his chest.

"We have to find cell service or a landline and call--" Julie started before she got cut off.

"I blame your asshole brother. It's not good enough he gets to show us up at his fucking mansion in Amber Lake, no. He has to one up *himself* and rent some fucking Swiss Family Robinson...goddamn *chalet* on top of a mountain and drag us--"

A gust of wind carrying a mountain's worth of snow dropped like a wool blanket over the road and the forest beyond. Nick switched the windshield wipers to full force but they were useless. And still the Caravan rolled forward, blind.

"Nick..." Julie whispered. "Please..."

"We don't even have enough gas." He said, glaring at her in the sickly green glow of the dashboard. "Have you even thought of that? We can't go back even if we wanted to."

And then a house appeared in the middle of the road.

Julie screamed and Nick's gaze snapped back toward the windshield as his foot crushed the brake pedal.

It wasn't a house. But it still filled the windshield as if they had driven straight into the side of a mountain.

The massive deer, a ten point buck, materialized out of the snow, standing stock still in the blizzard. Majestic, and directly in the Caravan's path.

Nick swore and cranked the wheel to the right but the van was moving too fast and the snow was too slippery, and the tires had long ago even thought of providing traction.

The van slid forward and clipped the front legs of the impressive beast. The deer back-peddled, its front hooves stomping down on the van grill and hood, denting it as easily as if it were made of tin foil.

The mini-van continued through its skid toward the right edge of the road. The tops of the frosted pine trees swayed and bent waving as if in greeting.

The guardrail screamed toward them and before Nick could do anything to prevent the inevitable, the van struck the barrier and tore through it with a shriek of ripping metal.

A moment later the van took a nose dive following the violent slope of the ground.

Julie screamed as the thick trunks of pine trees flew past their windows. Long branches with brittle fingers reached for them, scraping across their windows and slapping the doors as they plummeted down the rocky snow covered slope.

Terrified, Nick gripped the steering wheel doing what he could to steer around the boulders peeking out of the snow and the stumps of trees but his input was minimal. Even stomping on the brakes barely slowed them down. The van was moving too fast downhill and they were picking up speed rolling faster and faster and faster.

This could only end one way.

The Caravan began to slide sideways, the driver's side door angling toward downhill. The back wheels slammed into an unseen boulder in a loud gong and a shower of sparks that yanked a scream from Tara and Ozzy who were sitting straight in their seats, pale and sweating, clutching each other in a death grip.

A low hanging tree branch smashed into the windshield. The snow swept glass was replaced by a spiderweb of cracks and fissures.

The Caravan twisted toward the left and struck another hidden horror. A stump or a boulder. It didn't matter. But the impact rocked the van hard enough to shatter the already damaged windshield into a million pieces of glittering safety glass.

Nick and Julie did their best to turn away as the wave of glass swept over their faces, the bits tangling and catching in their hair and in the folds of their clothes. Wind and snow and ice barged greedily into the van forcing away any vestige of warmth from the interior.

The van continued to roll, slowly losing speed as the wonky flattened tires wobbled on its broken axle. A huge pine tree with a trunk wider than the front of the van loomed out of the darkness, caught in the glare of their remaining headlight. The Caravan struck the right side of the trunk. A glancing blow, but the vehicle spun in a tight circle and a moment later, slammed broadside into a boulder as large as a garden shed. Nick's driver side window exploded inward as the Caravan finally came to a stop with a bone-jarring jolt.

Bits of glass spun wildly through the interior of the van in the devil's idea of a snow globe as the safety belts snapped tight and the Jackson family was yanked backwards into their seats.

No one moved. No one spoke.

The only sound was the howl of the wind, the tinkling of glass and the ticking of the Caravan's engine as it quietly cooled before dying.

FIFTEEN

Nick awoke with a start, gasping, hauling in air and blinking wildly as if emerging not from unconsciousness, but from the bottom of an ocean crevasse. He opened his mouth but no words came. A bracing, white hot pain flared across his chest and stole his breath away.

Nick clawed at the seatbelt that had no doubt saved his life, but at the cost of his ribs, and unclipped the buckle. The relief was instant.

His face was wet and water was leaking into his eyes. He swiped it away with his right hand and even in the dying light he saw that his shaking fingers came away red with blood. His head rung like a bell. The pain was emanating from a spot just above his left temple where blood dripped down his cheek and slid down his neck.

With the tips of his bloody fingers he probed the area and winced. The skin was split and bleeding and there was a ping pong ball sized lump growing ever larger under his skin.

He added an aching left shoulder to the list of injuries as well as a coat that was nearly soaked through with a combination of blood and melting snow.

How long was I out?

As if a switch was flipped he remembered. The deer. The crash. He was not alone in the van. Julie. Tara. Ozzy.

Why weren't they saying anything?

Nick reached across to the passenger seat where Julie sat, slumped forward in her chair. Her blonde hair obscuring her face.

Was she breathing?

"*Julie!*" Nick yelled. "Julie!"

Knives stabbed through the gaps between his ribs with every word.

"Baby wake up!"

He couldn't reach her from where he sat, so he swiveled in his seat, glad to hear more sounds and moans coming from the back seat.

"Ozzy? Tara?" Nick said. "You guys all right?"

His heart swelled as they grunted their replies, but still Julie wasn't moving. Nick scrambled over the center console and gently lifted his wife's face and brushed aside the tangles of sweaty blonde hair that stuck to her face. It wasn't sweat he saw, sweeping more and more away from her scratched forehead and bleeding cheeks. It was blood.

"Julie." He said, shaking her shoulder, tears choking his throat. "Julie. Wake up."

"Mom?"

Ozzy's voice was so small and so close. Nick didn't need to see his son's face to know that his son would be a pale smear in the gloom. Tears spilling down his cheeks. His mouth a tight line.

Nick pressed two fingers to the side of his wife's throat like he'd seen in a million movies, not really sure if he was doing it right. He wasn't really sure about anything. His wife was the medical one. His wife was the calm one under pressure. His own heart banged painfully against his ribs and the blood from his head wound kept dripping into his eye.

"Is she all right?" Tara asked, shifting in the van, peering over the front seats.

Nick had no answers. No words.

"Julie." He said again. The single word a prayer, and a plea. *"Please."*

He held his wife's head in his hands, gently propping her up, brushing away the bits of glass caught in her hair and stuck to her cheeks, willing her to wake up.

And then, after what seemed like forever, she did.

Her eyes flickered to life. The lids fluttered and the eyeballs beneath darted left and right, while Nick, Tara and Ozzy held their collective breath.

She squinted once, grimacing in pain before she finally opened her eyes to the gloom of the Caravan interior. She stared blindly at her family huddled around her. Slowly, her eyes focused and found her children's faces scrubbed red from the cold.

"Are you okay?" Nick asked. Her gaze flicked to him

and she saw the left side of his face covered in dried streams of old blood.

"Oh Nick..." she whispered, sliding her palm over his cheek. "What happened?"

"It's okay." He told her, kissing her palm. "Can you move?"

"Are the kids okay?"

"We're okay." Tara replied, shifting in place. "Ozzy hit his head."

Immediately Julie found Ozzy in the dark.

"I'm fine, mom." Ozzy said, massaging the back of his head. "Just hurts."

"Good thing his head is solid rock." Tara said.

Nick ignored the kids and pulled his phone from his pocket and activated the flashlight. He swept the weak beam over his wife's body looking for blood.

"I think I'm all right." Julie said. "Maybe just blacked out. My head hurts, but I'm not bleeding."

Her voice was hoarse and too quiet. Her mouth and throat felt scraped raw and sore. She shifted in her seat and pain streaked across her chest between her breasts where the seatbelt cinched tight. She could actually feel the bruise forming a dark band across her flesh.

Blood dripped from Nick's forehead as he reached over and unclipped her seatbelt. Julie had to brace herself against the dash, but her legs and arms were unhurt. Immediately she turned backward in her seat to survey the children as Nick switched on the overhead dome light.

The kids looked so scared and young in the yellow

light, half buried under backpacks and books and twists of cables from their devices. Their eyes were bloodshot from crying and there was blood in Ozzy's thick dark hair.

"Oh my babies." Julie whimpered, before fresh tears came again. "Are you all right?"

"I hit the door." Ozzy said, his chin quivering. "My head hurts."

Neither could speak without crying. Ozzy struggled to undo his seatbelt and reach out for his mother.

"It's all right, baby." She told him and squeezed him over the seat in an awkward hug that both of them desperately needed.

"What happened, Dad?" Tara asked, as she pushed a backpack over her seat back and into the jumbled cargo space.

"There was a deer in the road." Nick told her. "I couldn't stop."

Tara nodded absently and peered out through her starred window and into the darkness of the forest. The snow had continued to fall and was quickly erasing the deep gouges in the snow made by the Caravan. In an hour the path they took down the mountainside would be entirely gone. As if they had never been here.

The dome light flickered, but stayed on as snow and wind whistled through the shifting pine trees. Soon the Caravan itself would be nothing more than a mound of white. Snow had begun to collect on the dashboard and the driver's side seat through the broken side window.

"Where are we?" Tara whispered, her breath smoking in the near dark.

CHAPTER
SIXTEEN

J ulie pulled Ozzy into the front seat with her and positioned his head under the dome light where she expertly parted his thick brown hair locating an angry laceration about half an inch wide. The boy winced as she probed, but she saw that the wound had already begun to stop bleeding.

"That hurts." Ozzy whined.

"I know, baby." She told him, smoothing back his hair and kissing him on the forehead. "It's gonna hurt for a while. You took quite a shot."

"How is he?" Nick asked, peering into his son's teary eyed face.

"He'll live." Julie said.

Nick moved his hand away from his own cut on his forehead and the blood began to flow again.

"Oh Jesus, Nick." Julie said, studying the wound just over Nick's left eye.

"Tara, see if you can reach the first aid kit in the back

there. It should be under the seat."

Nick checked the blood on his sleeve and shrugged. "It's not that bad, right?"

In the back seat Tara fished around through the old fast food wrappers and jumbled bits of luggage until she found the faded red First Aid bag her mom always insisted came with them on any trip. It wasn't standard issue, but filled with items she procured from the hospital where she worked as an emergency room nurse.

"Found it." Tara said, and handed her mom the beaten red bag.

"Thanks honey."

And then Julie turned her attention back to her husband.

"Did you black out at all?" Julie asked as she opened the bag and went to work slipping on latex gloves and digging through the contents of the bag until she found some absorbent gauze, alcohol and steri-strips.

"What?" Nick replied. "No. Maybe. I...I don't think so."

Julie gently grabs her husband's face and examines first his eyes and then the wound.

"Does your neck hurt?"

"No."

"Is Dad gonna be all right?" Ozzy asked, climbing over the back of the driver's seat and peering into the deep wound on his father's forehead.

"What?" Nick said, still pressing his sleeve to the bleeding wound "I'm fine, buddy."

"Nick, You gotta move your hand, honey." Julie

told him.

Nick moved his hand and using the edge of a bandage dipped in alcohol, Julie expertly cleaned the wound as Nick winced, and did his best not to move.

"Okay, don't move." She said as she peeled away the steri-strips and pinched the two ends of the wound together, sealing it closed as best she could.

"You're probably gonna have a scar." She whispered, their faces inches apart.

"Chicks dig scars, right babe?"

"Some do." Julie told him. Nick searched her face for a trace of a smile until Julie finally, gave him a little wink.

After Julie wiped the oozing blood away from the wound and then applied a gauze pad and some tape to hold the whole thing in place Nick asked, "Good?"

"Best I can do out here."

Nick took a second to take a peek at his wound and bandaged head in the rearview and then peered around at the faces of his family. All were pale and scared and a bit bloody in places.

They were all looking at him for the next step. The next play.

"It's getting cold in here." Tara said, wrapping her arms around herself.

"Do we have any gas left?" Julie asked. "Maybe if we can get the engine started we can block the windows with luggage or—

Nick slid behind the wheel and twisted the key still stuck in the ignition. The engine didn't even try. It didn't even make a sound. Not a single click. Just...*nothing*.

He tried it again with the same result and then climbed back onto his knees and swept his eyes over the family. As if on cue the overhead dome light flickered wildly and then went dark. All that remained was the ragged clouds of their breath touched with silver from the light of the waning moon.

"We can't stay here." Nick told them.

The way he saw it they had two options:

Option one was that they could bundle up, stay put and wait for daybreak. The cons of that plan was that the snow would continue to pile up and no one would come to find them and they might have to dig themselves out in the morning, that is if they lasted through the night without succumbing to hypothermia.

Option two was to climb back up the way they came and get back to the road and maybe wave down a snow-plow or find a house along the road.

"What are you talking about?" Julie asked.

"The van has no windows. No heat. We can't stay here."

"Where are we going to go?" Tara asked. "Are we near anything?"

"No." Julie said quickly. "We're not."

"That's not true." Nick said. "There were houses back along the road."

"What?" Julie asked. "What houses?"

"I saw the little green...*you know*...address signs."

"Where?"

"Back where we came."

"Nick." Julie said. She sounded exhausted. Wrung out. *"Please."*

"We can't stay here." He said. "We get up to the road. We find one of those houses and if no one is home, we... break a window and get inside. This is an emergency. We have no choice."

Tara and Ozzy stared back at him in the gloom. Their breath clouding the interior of the back seat as they waited for the adults to decide their fate.

"What if we don't find a house." Julie whispered, shifting closer to Nick. "We'll be out there with no protection. None and no way to find our way back."

"The temperature is already dropping in here. Soon we're going to get to the point where we can't keep warm. We have to make our move now. While we're still warm and have the strength."

"And your big plan is to start walking? In the dark?"

"There were houses back the way we came, Julie. Little green markers sticking out of the snow. I'm sure of it."

"I didn't see any markers." Julie said, searching his eyes. "And if we do this, there's no coming back. We strike out..." she cut her eyes to Ozzy and Tara waiting patiently, their eyes wet buttons in the dark, before lowering her voice so that only Nick could hear her. "We would be in serious trouble."

Nick held her gaze and she could feel his breath on her cheek.

"I know what I saw, Julie." He said, and prayed that he was telling the truth. "There's houses up there."

Julie stared at her husband for a long time before tipping her head in a slight nod. She opened her mouth to say okay, but her mouth had gone dry. She tried to look supportive, she tried to smile, but she was too scared.

Julie knew that if Nick was wrong and they didn't find shelter, they would die. The cold would wear them down until they became confused. They would get lost and then exhausted. Their bodies would eventually shut down and they would die.

Nick smiled and clapped his hands, startling her.

"Okay." He said. "It's going to be cold and we're going to be walking for a while so I need everyone to dress in layers. Snow pants, gloves, toques. Wear as much clothes as possible."

"Can we bring our bags?" Ozzy asked.

"Bring one bag with essentials, okay." Nick told them. "Clothes and small stuff. Leave everything else."

"What about the Christmas presents?" Tara said.

"Leave them." Nick said. "No one is gonna steal them out here."

"But—"

"We'll come back for them later on, okay? We'll figure it out."

"Dad?" Ozzy asked.

"Yeah, buddy."

"Can we go home now?"

Nick smiled and squeezed his son's shoulder over the seat.

"Ozzy." He said. "Abso-fucking-lutely."

SEVENTEEN

I t took a while navigating through the van, tilted as it was, but the Jacksons dug through their luggage, emptied backpacks and scoured the interior of the Caravan for fallen toques, missing gloves and winter boots. Finally, wrapped in every piece of winter gear they had brought, the Jackson family opened the rear cargo door and Julie and Nick followed their children out into the darkness.

In the end they didn't take much with them, Nick carried one backpack full of extra clothes and toiletries and Tara carried a second bag full of more clothes, Ozzy's tablet and Julie's worn first aid kit.

Nick pulled his phone from his pocket and once again activated the flashlight. Thick snowflakes landed on the screen, but Nick swept them away. In the weak light he could barely see the depressions the tires of the Caravan had made less than an hour ago, as it slid down the hill.

He found his direction and aimed for a pine tree that

had fallen, lying at a forty-five degree angle and then switched off the light to conserve the battery.

"Do we even know where we are?" Ozzy asked.

"First we need to get to the road. Okay?" Nick said, trying to sound as calm and relaxed as if they were completing a hike around the reservoir back home. "Come on. We'll be fine. Just watch your step."

Nick's first footstep sunk six inches into the snow and he nearly toppled forward. He quickly straightened and shot a grin over his shoulder at his nervously waiting family.

"Watch your step." He said. "Don't need anyone twisting an ankle."

He started again and soon he found his stride, picking up speed through the forest of creaking pines and evergreens shifting in place, their tops flicking left and right, caught in the whipping wind.

Nick flashed a smile back at his family as they trudged over his footsteps, desperate to keep up. Their faces hidden beneath scarves and hats.

"Come on. It'll be fine."

Nick leaned forward slightly as the slope angled sharply. His boots lost purchase on the frozen ground and he needed to grab a bare branch to stop himself from sliding backward.

"Slippery here." He said, a little breathlessly. "Gotta grab onto something."

He moved a few feet higher and then shifted track, finding a path that leveled out. Behind him Ozzy silently grabbed the branch he had used and followed his route. Behind his son, Julie and Tara picked their way up the slope, slipping and sliding, but climbing ever upward.

Slowly, the Jacksons climbed up the frozen slope, holding onto tree branches, climbing over boulders and sometimes, even crawling on all fours toward the narrow mountain road.

Nick lead the way but his cardio was never exceptional and he was nearly gassed about ten minutes in. Meanwhile, snow continued to fall and whip at their exposed cheeks and sting their eyes forcing them to tear.

Their gloved hands slipped over ice-laden rocks and their boots slid over the frozen ground. Ozzy cried out when he lost his footing and his right knee smashed into a rock half hidden in the snow. He lay there wailing until Julie reached him, assuring him that nothing was broken. Nick stood high above, trying to pick out the shadows of his family as they stood, and continued to climb.

Since beginning the climb Nick hadn't stopped wondering if he made the right choice; that he actually did see the green address markers sticking out of the snow and it wasn't just a trick of his memory.

Nick leaned against the bare trunk of a massive ever-green and stared up at the slope. Even in the filtered moonlight he could see the path of destruction brought by their vehicle. Deep gouges carved in the ground, chunks ripped out of tree trunks and bits of red plastic and weather stripping left behind.

He tried to control his breathing, gathering his strength for what he hoped would be the final push.

"You see anything?" Julie asked. Nick had been lost in thought. He didn't hear his family crunching up through the snow until they were a few feet away.

"How much longer?" Ozzy asked, the sound of his voice drawn out into a whine.

"Almost at the top, buddy." Nick told him. "Not far now."

He saw that Julie had another question, but Nick had no more answers. They were committed now. They had to get to the top. That was step one.

Nick turned and grabbed the next handhold, a twisted root arcing out of the pristine snow and pulled himself higher up the slope. Behind him his family marched silently forward. Snow crunching beneath boots, grunts, heavy breathing and whispered curses higher and higher until...

"Thank God." Nick whispered.

He saw the flattened edge of the roadway and a glint of twisted metal beyond.

"We did it, guys!" Nick said, with barely enough breath in his lungs to get the words out. "Right up there."

Nick found a little gas left in the tank and with his lungs burning, he pushed through the last hundred feet and scrambled on all fours up to the road.

Reaching up, he gripped the scarred wooden post that supported the bent-to-hell guardrail and pulled himself up until he was finally standing on even ground.

The pristine mountain road stretched left and right disappearing into the darkness. Any tire tracks left by the Caravan had long since been obscured by the falling snow. But what troubled him more, was that there were no other tracks. None. Which meant no one, not even plows traveled this road.

"Dad?" Ozzy said. "Where are we going now?"

Nick returned to the edge of the slope and helped his son climb up to the road and then watched as Julie and Tara followed close behind, using branches and jutting rocks as hand holds to reach the summit.

Ozzy stood in the center of the road and turned in place. There was nothing but darkness out here. In every direction.

There was no light except the moon that was hidden behind the gauze of clouds. No warm yellow glow from nearby houses. Definitely no street lights. He had been camping once a few years ago with his dad, but other than those two nights in Yellowstone, he had never known darkness like this could exist.

"Dad?" Ozzy said. "I don't see a light."

"That's okay." He said, as he helped Julie and then Tara get to the road. Their labored breathing steaming out through the scarves wrapped around their mouths.

"No lights, Nick." Julie said. "You said you saw houses."

"I said I saw markers." Nick told her. "Maybe no one is home."

It had to be here, Nick thought. *Please God let me be right about this.*

"Dad, I don't see it." Ozzy told him, as he moved further down the road. "I don't see it. I don't see anything."

Nick didn't see anything either. Just snow and more fucking trees. But it had to be there. He hadn't imagined it. He didn't.

"Nick?"

He stomped past his wife without replying and made his way further down the road, the way they had come. There had to be a marker. A house.

There fucking had to be.

He should have come up here himself and checked it out. Now if there was no marker, then, the best thing would be to go back to the van and huddle until morning and then pray all over again that this road was actually plowed.

Who knew the roads wouldn't be plowed. He sure didn't. He didn't live out here in the boondocks like some animal. Where he lived there was power and heat and hot meals delivered to your house anytime of the day or night.

He stomped further down the road, following the bend as it wound to the right around a copse of trees.

His feet ached, his head throbbed. He spun in place as he shuffled further down the road.

"Nick." Julie called, sounding farther away. "Where are you going?"

"Come on." He called to her, and waved them to follow. "Come on."

"There had to be. There had to be. It had to be there." Nick was chanting now, willing this marker into existence. It had to be there. He stomped through the blowing drifts and kicked aside a chunk of ice that no doubt fell off his own vehicle. He cleared the shifting trees around the bend and...

...there was nothing.

CHAPTER
EIGHTEEN

Nick pushed himself further, and further, almost jogging at times following the road, eyes forward, squinting through the sting of the ice pellets and razored wind. Behind him his family called out to him, begging him to slow down, to wait. But wait for what?

The road dipped and curled around the rocky outcropping as the snow continued to fall and the wind continued to howl. Tara and Ozzy were both crying. Whimpering in their snowsuits. They were city kids used to cold snaps that sent alerts to their phones and where they always had the option of staying indoors. It was just a stroke of luck that they had found the kids snow gear buried deep in the back of their storage unit in the hopes of a skiing adventure.

Ahead the road coiled out in front of them and it felt as though they were spiralling down the mountain. Or was he climbing higher? Nick stopped and stared up the slope and the twisting trees. What the hell?

He felt blood from his head wound leaking down the side of his face and soaking his toque.

"Nick." Julie snapped. "*Wait.*"

"What?"

"Where are you going?"

"What are you talking about?" Nick shouted over the wind. "There's houses —"

"Where, Nick?" Julie said exasperated. "Where? I don't see anything. There's nothing up here."

Nick slowed and stopped and swept his gaze over the clutch of his family huddled together behind him in a shivering mass. Julie had her arms wrapped around Ozzy and Tara had her head hidden from the wind behind Julie's shoulder.

"We have to go back." Julie said.

"Back? Back to what? The van?"

"I don't know, but the kids are freezing. I'm freezing. We don't know what you saw or where we're going."

"We gotta keep going, a little while longer." Nick told her. "I saw it."

"Dad, please." Tara moaned. "My feet are frozen."

"We can't stop now, honey." Nick said, and pulled his daughter into a hug, rubbing her back through her ski jacket. "We gotta keep going, just a little while longer. I promise. We're almost there."

"H-How do you know?"

"Come on, Ozzy, let's go." He said. "Team Jackson."

"Ten more minutes, Nick." Julie said, exhausted.

"Then what?"

"We go back to the van."

"Why?" Nick asked. "You wanna climb back down the slope to the busted van with no windows? That's your plan?"

"It's better than wandering around out here." Julie snapped back. "There's nothing out here."

"There's a house."

"Where, Nick?" Julie said. "Where is it? At least in the van we're out of the elements."

"Barely."

"I'm sorry, but this didn't work." Julie said. "Ten more minutes and then I'm calling it."

"Maybe we need to go straight up on this side." Nick told her. Staring up at the side of the mountain that angled nearly straight up from the road.

"No, Nick. No."

"Why?"

"Because we barely made it up the slope from the van." Julie said. "That looks insane and we don't even know what's up there."

"Come on then." He said and shuffled away through the storm, following the road.

Nick picked up speed and shut the rest of the world out. The only sound was the crunch of his boots in the snow and the wheeze of his breath. He had to find it. He had to find something. If not a house, a barn or anything, even another abandoned car would work at this point.

Behind him he thought he heard his name carried on the wind. He shot a glance back and saw his family had fallen behind. A hundred feet back they were flickers of color in the wall of white.

Nick stood in the middle of the pristine road. Their tire tracks were long gone and so was any other sign that anyone, ever, travelled this road.

Still he kept moving. Putting one boot in front of the other. He raised his head and scanned the trees bending beside the road, the ragged rocks sticking out of the mountainside to his right and knew he had failed.

There was no house out here.

No barn.

Nothing.

As if on cue, clouds heavy with snow shifted overhead and blotted out whatever moonlight hung above them. Darkness fell like a final curtain and Nick skidded to a stop on the icy road.

He put his hands on his knees and felt like he was going to throw up. He was lost. They were lost. He had lead them up the mountain slope to a spot that was even more dangerous.

He was done.

He could feel the greasy diner cheeseburger slosh around in his belly and he could taste it in the back of his throat.

Behind him his family's footsteps crunched in the snow, getting closer. Soon they would be close enough to ask him what they should do next. He had no idea.

He straightened and turned to face them. He saw the disappointment in Julie's eyes. It was a familiar look that he recognized. She knew without asking that he had failed. It broke his heart to see her shoulders slump. Her eyes flicked around the snowy road lined with shifting trees. Looking at anything but him.

"Dad...?" Tara asked, almost afraid to finish her thought.

Nick opened his mouth to speak when Ozzy yelled from behind them. He had passed Nick's position on the road, continuing further into the blinding blizzard.

"Dad." He said, trundling off down the road, his voice carried on the icy wind.

"Ozzy." Nick called to him. "Where are you going? Come back."

"I'm freezing." Ozzy said, his voice barely above a whisper. "What are you waiting for?"

Nick, Julie and Tara shared a look and then jogged to catch up to the little man marching along, cutting thin parallel ruts in the snow with his boots.

"Where are you going?" Tara said, reaching for Ozzy's shoulder and spinning him around. "Stop."

"The marker." Ozzy said. "Like dad said."

Nick's head snapped up and scanned the side of the road as the wind howled again. The trees that bordered the road shifted in place and there it was.

He hadn't imagined it.

It was there.

A goddamn green address marker sticking out of the snow. Nick stepped closer and wiped his hand over the number plate revealing the address printed in reflective white numbers:

4907

Nick grabbed the tiny metal marker, squeezing his fingers around its edges to make sure he wasn't imagining it. He found Julie's green eyes above the scarf and below the edge of her toque. He could tell she was smiling.

They were saved.

CHAPTER
NINETEEN

The Jacksons felt the gravel of the driveway crunch under their boots as they climbed the gentle rise. They moved huddled together, a frightened herd with Nick in the lead. Fifty feet from the road, at the crest of the hill, the dark blur of the cabin swam into view.

Nick picked up the pace. There was a half buried pick up truck parked out front, but there were no lights on in the cabin. No smoke from the chimney. The place looked deserted, but he didn't care. It had four walls and a roof, and that was enough for him.

Behind the small bungalow tall pines shook and bent in the wind. Beyond that screen of frosted trees a great flat wall of rock rose through the rags of low slung clouds and blotted out the stars. Nick felt as though he had reached the edge of the world.

Nick herded his family past the pick up and up the three steps to the cabin's wraparound porch. Snow had drifted against the front door nearly reaching the dull brass door knob. Nick peered through the tiny square windows and scanned the dark interior. No movement. No lights. Not even an ember in the stone fireplace set against the far wall.

With a gloved fist he knocked hard enough to rattle the door in its frame.

"*Easy*, Nick." Julie said. "You're gonna scare the hell out of them."

"You want to stand out here all night?" He shot over his shoulder.

He moved along the length of the porch trying to peek into the next window but heavy curtains blocked his view. He stood on his tiptoes, but it didn't help.

He returned to the front door and knocked again. Louder. Harder. No one stumbled out of bed, bleary eyed to investigate. Nothing. No movement at all.

"Hello?" Nick shouted through the tiny squares of glass.

"Is it locked?" Tara asked.

Nick shot a look at his daughter as if to say, *'of course it's locked.'* and then tried the handle. The knob turned easily and the door swung inward with tiniest squeak of its hinges.

Nick smiled and slowly stepped inside.

"Good call, honey."

"Wait…" Julie said, but he was already across the threshold. Tara moved to join her father inside but Julie snagged her coat from behind and held her where she was.

"What?" Tara said. "I'm freezing."

"Just wait for a second. There could be some old couple in there sleeping. Everyone out here has a gun."

"For real, Mom?"

"For real." She said. "Just wait."

Tara huffed and stomped her feet to stay warm. Ozzy stood in front of his mother, with her arms wrapped around him, keeping him close. He craned his neck as much as he could to peer into the house through the open door.

Inside the cabin was barely warmer than outside, but at least Nick was out of the wind. He pulled his iPhone from his pocket and activated the flashlight app. Its beam barely lit the three feet in front of him but it was something.

He found himself in what appeared to be the main room of the cabin. To his right against the wall was a kitchen with a small electric stove and a sink. Dirty dishes crusted with moldy food were piled on the counter and in the sink itself.

The fireplace that he spied through the door was dark and cold. A threadbare couch piled with pillows and the twist of a blanket sat in front of it.

He moved deeper into the room and passed a scarred wooden table that had been used as a workstation. The table was nearly buried under an ancient MacBook, newspaper clippings and loose pages torn from an artist's sketch pad. Nick didn't touch anything but it was obvious that most of the drawings depicted the same thing. A thin naked woman.

The drawings were proficient, the work on the woman's form was done with care, but where the artist lacked strength was the woman's face.

In every drawing the woman's features were drawn slightly out of proportion. Her dark eyes a little too dark and almost feline in their depiction. The edges of her mouth, her thin lips and the tiny sharp teeth hidden behind gave the woman an animalistic look.

The woman looked dangerous. Feral.

Nick stared at a sketch dominated by the woman's face. Her eyes were shiny black buttons glaring out from behind a curtain of greasy hair.

"Fucking creepy." He muttered.

"Nick?" Julie asked from the doorway. "You all right?"

Something about the drawings gave him pause. Surely they were just drawings. Sketches. The doodles of a deranged pervert, who might be lying dead somewhere in the back rooms of this very cabin.

If he was dead, it would explain why the truck was left behind.

"Yeah." He said quickly, shooting his wife a strained smile. "Just gonna check the back rooms. You guys stay there, okay?"

Julie gave him a quick nod and he saw from her expression that she felt it too. Something was off.

Nick forced his feet to move. One step. And then another. Until he was shuffling deeper into the cabin. A thin line of sweat trickled down between his shoulder blades as he entered a short hallway.

The first door on his left lead to a tiny bathroom.

107

Shower, toilet, sink. He pushed the door left ajar all the way open and made sure no one was hiding in the stand up shower stall, or had collapsed next to the toilet. Satisfied, he stepped back into the hall.

Two doors left.

A warning flashed across his iPhone letting him know that he had less than 10% battery power left. He dismissed the alarm and aimed his flashlight at the next door on his left. It too was left halfway open.

"Hello?"

No response.

Somehow that was worse.

"Is anybody home?" Nick hissed, his voice just above a whisper.

Nick wasn't good with death. The last time he saw a dead body was Grandma Linda back in Chicago. He was eleven. He had waited in a slowly shuffling line to her casket behind his quietly weeping mother and father, behind uncles and aunts he barely knew in order to pay his final respects.

When he finally reached the coffin his Grandma was there. But also not there. It looked like her body, but the face was painted like a doll. Rosy cheeks and glossy red lips. Still, her hands looked the same. Plump and pink. They were the hands that made cookies and the short stubby fingers that tickled him breathless.

He focused on her hands and the way, even now, she smelled of old flowers. He whispered his goodbye and reached out, and touched her hand wrapped in her favorite rosary. Her flesh was cold modeling clay beneath

A DARK BREED

his fingertips. He could feel the ends of his fingers sinking in, touching frozen bones.

Clutching his phone in his right hand he eased open the door and found himself in a small bedroom.

A whispered prayer smoked from his lips as he searched around the empty bed. The sheets and blankets lay more or less flat in a messy tangle. No one was hiding beneath the covers, or around the bed.

A plastic baby monitor sat dark and weirdly out of place.

What the fuck?

Was there a baby here?

An overstuffed chair sat in the corner buried beneath a pile of clothes. Nick nudged the pile with the toe of his boot, ensuring no one was hiding beneath.

He did a final sweep of the floor and finding no bodies, dead or otherwise, he let out the breath he was holding.

One room left.

Nick crossed the hall and eased open the door to the final room. It was smaller than the bedroom and stacked with heavy duty plastic crates. Stencilled on the side was the name: PROFESSOR HAROLD MARKS.

Nick opened the first one on the floor and found it was filled with food supplies. A case of ramen noodles sat on top and beneath that he found bags of oatmeal, sugar, coffee, pasta sauce, dried pasta, etc.

He set the lid down and swept his light over the rest of the room. At the back of the wall, beside a tower built with cases of frozen water bottles was a green metal gun case with its door left ajar. Nick eased open the door and found a small arsenal inside.

A black pump action shotgun stood next to an older, lever action shotgun, and resting on a shelf in front of a wall of boxed ammunition, lay a single black handgun. It was heavier than Nick imagined. He handled it delicately, at arms length gripping it around the slide with his gloved hand. On the side of the weapon the word GLOCK was stamped into the metal.

What the hell?

CHAPTER

TWENTY

"Nick?", Julie asked weakly from the doorway.
"Nick?"

"Come on, mom. We're freezing." Tara whined.

Julie finally conceded and pulled her children into the cabin and shut the door behind them. With the door closed the silence inside the cabin made their ears ring. They were out of the wind but their breath still smoked in the freezing cabin.

"Nick?" Julie tried again.

No response.

Julie tried the wall switch. Nothing. No power. Still she spotted the dirty dishes in the sink. Food left out on the counter that had once been some sort of meat had gone rotten.

"Don't touch anything." Julie warned her children who had quietly drifted through the main living area, exploring their new environs.

Julie's face was set in a tense expression as she peered down the hallway and called for Nick again.

"It's fine." He said, stomping back down the hall. "There's no one here."

"Okay."

Tara moved to the work station and flipped open the dead laptop.

"Tara, what did I just say? Don't touch anything."

"I don't think anyone has been here in a while, Mom."

"I checked everywhere." Nick said. "There's nobody here. No power either."

"*Perfect*." Tara said. "Amazing."

"You wanna still be outside?" Nick said quickly. "Be my guest."

"You think there's a generator?" Julie asked.

"I don't know." Nick told her. "Maybe. There's a fireplace though. I'll see if I can get it started. At least get some heat in here."

"Did you see a phone?" Tara asked.

"No, honey."

"I didn't see any phone lines either." Ozzy told them.

"Let me get the fire going." Nick told them. "Get some heat, warm us up, okay? There's some supplies in the back. We'll be fine."

WHILE OZZY STUDIED a small stack of books left on the floor near the couch, Nick scoured the place for paper garbage he could burn. He wanted to burn the eerie drawings of the woman, but in the end he couldn't do it. He settled on gathering them into a pile and stacking them facedown beneath the useless laptop. Instead he found an old local newspaper, *The Whistler,* dated July 17th on the kitchen counter.

Two lonely sticks of firewood stuck from the metal basket next to the fireplace, but it was a start. There had to be more outside or in a shed somewhere on the property. Right now he was just happy to be indoors and moments away from providing some sort of comfort to his family as they huddled under a blanket behind him on the couch.

Just as his dad had taught him, Nick crumpled up the newspaper into loose balls and arranged them beneath a few twigs he scrounged around the remnants of the last fire and used Julie's lighter to spark the thing up. Fire spread through the paper quickly, gobbling up all the fuel. Nick angled the two pieces of wood in a steep triangle above the rising flame and hoped for the best.

"Do you think the owner will be pissed when he comes back?" Tara asked.

"He could've died." Ozzy said, holding up a battered copy of a book called *Winter Hunter*. "Out in the forest. He looks pretty old."

Ozzy turned the book over and the glossy author picture on the back of the dust jacket showed Professor Harold Marks standing in front of some ragged mountain. By the looks of the lush green vegetation, probably somewhere tropical. He wore a beige bush cap over a faded PEPSI t-shirt, cargo shorts and hiking boots. Next to him stood a stern looking black man who stared at the camera with an expression that bordered on hostility.

Julie reached for the book and turned it over in her hands.

"Professor Harold Marks."

"His name is on a bunch of crates in the back." Nick said. "This must be his cabin."

"So cool." Ozzy said.

"Well, we'll just make a list of all the things we use and send him a check if he doesn't show up or...whatever." Julie announced to the group, handing the book to Tara.

"Who is he?" Tara asked.

"He's a cryptozoologist." Ozzy explained.

"In English."

"He studies weird phenomena and strange animals. Like giant squids and urban legends. I read this book, *Winter Hunter*."

"Of course you did." Tara said, tossing it back to her little brother.

"It was about the Sasquatch. Although they call it Yeti where he went. He spent a year in Nepal hunting for it."

"Did he find it?" Julie asked.

"No. But he found a bunch of huge teeth and footprints. The book was still super cool."

"So he's a crazy person." Tara told him.

"Why would you say that?" Ozzy said.

"Because he's a grown man who spent a year of his

life hunting a fictional monster. They lock people up for doing weird shit like that."

"Tara. Language." Julie snapped.

Nick shifted the position of the wood in the hearth and smiled as the tinder finally caught crackling and snapping. He basked in the heat for as long as he could stand it and then stood and stretched. His lower back cracked and popped.

"How's your head?" Julie asked.

"Feels like I took a right hook from Mike Tyson, but I'll live. How you doin'?"

Julie shrugs.

"It's not the worst Christmas vacation I've been on." She said.

Nick and Julie laughed and it felt good to smile. Felt like forever since it had happened at the diner. A lifetime ago.

"While I'm outside can you see if you guys can find a phone or keys for that truck." Nick asked them.

"Where are you going?" Tara asked.

"That's the last of the wood and it's not gonna last long. I'm gonna see if there's a wood pile or maybe even a generator I can get going. Something."

"Be careful."

Next to the door he spied a bulky flashlight with a pistol grip. He thumbed the power button and to his surprise a strong purple beam sparked to life.

"Weird." He said, sweeping the strange light over the cabin.

"Why is it purple?" Julie asked.

"That's so cool." Ozzy said. "It's a UV flashlight."

"A what?"

"Ultraviolet."

"Why would he have an ultraviolet flashlight?" Tara asked.

TWENTY-ONE

N ick had enjoyed the brief reprieve from the cold so close to the flames. Bathed in the radiant heat, the feeling had returned to his cheeks and the tip of his nose and he could feel the blood running through his fingers again.

Now, standing by the front door of the little cabin he could feel the cold creeping back, freezing his clothes and settling in his bones. Through the tiny square windows he could see that the snow had slowed a bit, but it was the relentless wind that presented the problem. From where he stood the pickup truck was a vague dark blur where it sat less than twenty feet away.

Grumbling, he yanked his sodden wool toque from his pocket and pulled it down over his head. He followed that up with his gloves that were, no surprise, still wet, and reached for the door knob.

Nick opened the cabin door and a gust of icy wind cut right through his clothes and bled away whatever warmth he had stored. Lowering his head to his chest to keep his face away from the barrage of icy pellets, Nick stepped onto the porch and slammed the door behind him, cutting off a current of swirling snow.

Just find some wood and get back in.

How hard would that be?

Outside, away from the modest light of the fire, he had only the moonlight filtered through the storm. He blinked, getting his bearings and then groped for the railing of the porch. Keeping one hand on the rail, he slowly made his way a few feet at a time in the dark, buffeted by blowing snow, before he remembered he had brought a flashlight with him. Blindly, he thumbed the ON switch and immediately the intense beam of purple light speared through the gloom.

It was such a weird thing to have. Nick thought. The only other time he had seen a UV light being used in real life was on those news expose of dirty hotel rooms. Inevitably, the on-the-street reporter would wave the beam over the bed sheets and the floor of some bargain basement motel showing the rapt viewers the dried remnants of blood and semen and God knew what else.

His hand slid along the railing, making his way past the dark window of the professor's bedroom, until he found the corner and turned right where the porch ended in the shorter section of an 'L'.

The purple beam found a large black generator that stood silent next to a small wooden enclosure designed to keep a stockpile of chopped wood out of the elements. Thankfully, the rack was half full.

At least they wouldn't freeze to death. Nick thought.

Nick kicked at the top three pieces of firewood buried under a tiny drift of snow and welded together by a layer of ice. When they finally broke apart Nick stacked them neatly next to the generator.

The wind tossed a fistful of icy pellets at his face, stinging the exposed skin around his eyes.

"I blame you Richie." He muttered. "You and your stupid Alpine Christmas. Fucking idiot."

When he had all the wood he could carry stacked in a neat pile, Nick shuffled around the tiny space, probing the darkness behind the generator and on the opposite side of the wood box and found nothing except an empty gas can, probably meant for the generator.

"You gotta be fucking kidding me."

Nick shined the weird light out onto the rear yard, painting the nearby trees in violet, looking for a shed or an outbuilding. Something. He had searched the entire cabin and as far as he could see there wasn't a basement or crawl space where the old professor would store gas or more firewood. The only reasonable option would be to have a...

Nick's light played over a depressed track about four feet wide that lead from the far end of the driveway, the end closest to the mountain and the forest beyond. The path wasn't marked or groomed other than it looked too straight to be anything other than man made.

He grabbed the three pieces of firewood and the empty gas can and hurried back to the front door of the cabin.

Inside his family had moved the couch closer to the fireplace and he found them all huddled beneath the single blanket. Julie sat in the middle, her head resting on Tara's shoulder while Ozzy struggled to read one of the professor's books in the dying firelight.

Nick stomped over to the fire and arranged three of the pieces of wood he brought in as best he could. Snow and ice sizzled in the flames sending up clouds of steam. The rest he piled nearby on the hearth to dry out.

"At least there's wood." Julie said.

"There's enough." Nick told her.

"What do you mean?"

"I mean we have enough for a while." He told her. "He had one of those wood holder-thingies at the end of the porch, but it was only half full."

In the weak light Julie's face looked gray with worry, her eyes ringed with dark smudges.

"What do we do if..."

"I think there's a shed or something deeper in the forest." Nick said, cutting her off. "I'm gonna go and check it out. I found a generator but it's out of gas. Maybe he's got more in there."

"Do you want me to —"

But he cut her off again with a shake of his head.

"It's okay." He said. "Stay here, get warm. I'll be right back."

"Watch out for the wolves, Dad." Ozzy said, never glancing up from his book. "There's tons of them out there."

"Thanks, buddy."

Julie watched him go, her anxiety pinching her features until the door slammed behind him. She listened until his heavy footsteps clunked down the three porch steps and then he was gone.

A pit opened up in her stomach and she suddenly knew...with absolute certainty, she would never see him again.

TWENTY-TWO

O utside again in the freezing cold, Nick grumbled and switched on the UV flashlight.

Fucking wolves...thanks Ozzy...

As if he didn't have enough to worry about, he had to keep his head on a swivel for man-eating wolves the size of Bengal tigers creeping around out here in the dark.

He shook his head and high stepped to the end of the driveway and the beginning of the path. Nick stomped through the knee high snow and soon found himself inside a grove of pine trees. At least beneath their canopies he was protected from the worst of the blowing snow and the razored wind.

Here the beaten down path was littered with the remnants of boot prints and fallen pine needles, a stark contrast to the rest of the white landscape.

Nick aimed his light ahead and spotted the low slung bunker. It definitely didn't look like a shed. The walls were made of heavy timbers and there were no windows that Nick could see.

The violet beam glinted off the edge of a central metal door that had been left ajar. The door was painted in streaks of green and brown in an attempt to blend in with the surroundings. It definitely didn't feel like a shed. A shed was a place you kept your lawnmower, maybe some deck chairs. This place looked like it was built for an entirely different reason. This place looked like a bomb shelter or the bunker of a doomsday prepper.

The way it was built against the rock face, hidden by a screen of trees and deliberately camouflaged gave Nick a sinking feeling. He slowed his shuffle until he was entirely stopped. Snow spiraled through the purple beam and gathered on his shoulders as he studied the heavy metal door left open, and the two sliding bolts used to secure it.

What the hell...

Snow had begun to drift against the door and whoever had made those bootprints had either been here a long time ago, or had remained inside and not closed the door. His deduction didn't help overcome his fear. He felt himself rooted in place for no real reason except a gut feeling that was telling him. Screaming at him: DO NOT GO IN THERE.

Why would he go in there? They had enough firewood. For a while, he added to himself. They needed the generator to power their phones, to call for help. He needed to go in there.

He swung his light up and swept the beam over the

surrounding forest, and the swaying trees until finally he shined his light on the door once more.

He still felt conflicted.

More like terrified.

"Fuck." He muttered. "Fuck it."

He took a few steps forward, grabbed the vertical door handle and pulled the door open. The door belonged on a submarine and creaked just as much as he wrenched it open, its rusted hinges screaming the entire time.

Nick took one step inside, aiming his light into the darkness when the warm fetid air washed over him. The rancid stink of body odor and filth. The reek of vomit and shit rushed out from the dark and forced him to scramble back, away from the door.

Hands on his knees, Nick gagged and tasted bile at the back of his throat. He spat out a mouthful of stomach acid and worked on slowing his breathing.

What the actual fuck?

There was something dead in there. He was certain. *At least one something,* he thought. It could have been a mass grave and Nick wouldn't have doubted it. The stink was that palpable.

He reached down into the snow between his boots where he had dropped the UV flashlight and scooped it up. He brushed the snow from the lens and saw that it was still working. Nick pulled up his scarf and wound it around his face, covering his nose and mouth before turning back to the bunker door.

At the doorway, Nick angled the beam into the

bunker and illuminated the right side of the interior. In the far corner a computer desk was set up topped with two monitors. An old school CPU tower sat below the desk with all the associated cables and wires running across the floor to a generator identical to the one he had seen up on the porch.

What the hell would you need computer equipment out here for?

More, thicker cables snaked from the generator across the floor, to the left side of the bunker. From where Nick stood he couldn't see where the wires ended. He had to get closer. He had to step inside.

The reek of whatever was in there forced Nick to hold a gloved hand over his nose as he eased through the doorway, keeping the purple beam up and ready, guiding his way. The smell stung his eyes but he kept moving forward, the interior of the bunker coming into view.

Three feet inside Nick froze.

His light shook in his hand as the beam played over the handmade bars of the prison cage and the thin form a dead woman lying inside.

"Holy shit..."

TWENTY-THREE

Inside the cabin Julie made the executive decision to pile every piece of wood Nick had brought inside onto the fire. Soon their dwindling little campfire was raging, cracking and snapping sparks onto the edge of their blankets. Bright tongues of red and orange leapt out of the hearth and threatened to singe their eyebrows forcing them to move the couch back a few feet.

With their mood slightly buoyed by the rising temperature in the cabin, their rumbling stomachs lead them to the small kitchen where they began to raid the cabinets with abandon.

Whoever the professor was he definitely wasn't here, and he wasn't coming back any time soon with his truck half buried in the driveway. Not that anyone could drive safely in the storm. And surely, he wouldn't begrudge them for dipping into a few of his supplies to feed some hungry children.

Truth be told, Julie didn't give a shit if he did mind. After surviving the car crash and then crawling up the mountain slope she might never get the cold out of her bones and she was absolutely starving.

Tara was a the first to find something decent. A box of stale off brand chocolate chip cookies. Ozzy silently appeared at her elbow, pleading eyes of a Basset hound staring up at her.

"Find your own." Tara told him.

"Tara." Her mother said. "Come on."

With a sigh Tara handed the box to her little brother who slammed his fist into the carton and pulled out a handful of the crumbling cookies. Julie plucked one from his palm and popped it into her mouth, instantly regretting it.

"I hate to say it." Tara said around a mouthful of cookie. "But this is still better than Christmas with Uncle Rich."

Julie laughed and coughed out a spray of cookie bits.

"You're awful." Julie said.

"So are these cookies." Tara said, pulling a can of Coke from the fridge and popping the top.

"Is there any more?" Julie asked.

Tara opened the fridge door wider and Julie spotted a few cans of beer, a carton of milk that had turned to yoghurt and little else.

"Great."

They passed the last can around until it was gone and then Julie clapped her hands, feeling a little better. A little more energized from the sugar and the caffeine.

"All right," She said. "We need to find the keys to the truck or a phone, okay?"

The kids nodded and gave her a weak smile.

"The sooner we do that, the sooner we can go home."

JULIE FOUND the battery powered lantern on the professor's desk and snapped it on. Carrying it with her she started her search in the master bedroom at the end of the hall.

She set the lantern down on the bedside table and shook the twisted sheets hoping to hear the tell-tale jingle of keys, but heard nothing. All she got for her efforts was a cloud of old sweat and nicotine. It reminded her of her chain smoking grandfather who she and her brothers were forced to visit every Sunday when they were kids.

The old man always wore the same ratty blue cardigan. Probably never changed it and washed it even less. He smelled like this room. For a moment she was back there, on her grandfather's lap. Yellow nicotine stained fingers pinching her cheeks, the smell of unwashed skin and old smoke. She let the sheets flop back to the bed and wiped her hands over the front of her jeans.

She moved away from the bed and opened the single closet which was entirely empty save for a single garment bag, the kind of cheap plastic cover you get at the dry cleaners. A dark brown or black suit hung on the hook complete with a starched white shirt and black tie

128

already knotted at the throat. She checked the receipt still clipped to the bag. It was from July.

There wasn't much on the floor. A pile of clothes had been dumped on the overstuffed chair, and she was loathe to pick through them, but she did her best. Shaking pairs of jeans and hooded sweatshirts, but found nothing in the pockets.

She moved on to the bedside table and found a white plastic baby monitor. The monitor was attached to a cable that ran to the wall. A thin, white cable neatly stapled to follow the edge of the baseboard where it disappeared into a tiny hole in the wall near the corner of the room.

Julie pressed her face against the bedroom window in an attempt to follow the trajectory of the wire, but after it left the house she lost sight of it.

Why does he have a baby monitor?

Just the sight of it dropped her core temperature. He was listening to something. To *someone.* Her breath caught in her throat. Her eyes pinned to the window and the swirling darkness beyond.

Did he have a baby out there?

Julie shook her head, banishing the awful thought. Her fingers trembled as she reached to switch on the monitor. The green power light switched on, but nothing else. She leaned closer to the microphone set into the base of the device but heard only static. For a few breathless moments she waited...wondering what she would do if she heard a baby cry...or worse...a voice call out.

Nothing happened.

She switched off the unit and let out a shuddering breath.

She needed to calm down. But more importantly, they needed to get out of here.

With the unit switched off she restarted her search and opened the small bedside table. There was only one drawer. Inside she found a handful of change, some spare batteries, probably for the baby monitor and a collection of pill bottles all prescribed to Harold Marks.

Julie read the labels: XANAX, CODEINE, PERCOCET, VALIUM.

"Thank God." Julie whispered and opened the bottle of Valium. She shot a glance over her shoulder making sure her daughter was still in the spare bedroom across the hall, and dry swallowed the little yellow pill.

She capped the bottle and stuffed the rest of the drugs back into the drawer, out of sight.

She took a second for herself, her eyes closed, and focused on her breathing, as the tiny little pill worked its magic into her bloodstream.

When she could no longer feel the drumbeat of her heart in her ears she opened her eyes.

She took a slow even breath, and then Tara began to scream.

TWENTY-FOUR

urther down the hall Tara made quick work of the disgusting bathroom finding nothing of interest other than a seriously dirty sink, and a worse looking shower, absolutely festering with mold and mildew, and then moved on to the spare bedroom.

She wrenched open the first plastic crate and found a Costco sized box of protein bars and ramen and other dried goods.

At least we're not going to starve.

She moved aside the cases containing food to uncover a larger case that looked different from the rest. This one was a large black rectangle with silver metal adorning the corners. It looked like the cases the school band used to transport their instruments, just more fancy.

She found the clasps and expected to find maybe a guitar or a violin. Definitely not an array of bleached skulls nestled in custom cut styrofoam.

"Oh Jesus Christ." Tara said. "Mom! *Mom!*"

Tara heard her mother's hurried footsteps charge across the hall, the lantern swinging from her hand splashing shadows over the walls. A second later she was standing over her as Tara pulled one of the skulls from the case.

"What the hell? Don't touch it." Julie warned, but it was too late.

Tara held what looked like the skull of an ape in her small hands. The sloping forehead and the large rounded teeth gave it the look of some sort of primate, or primitive man.

"Is that human?" Julie asked, as she pointed to another skull still in the case. It certainly looked human. The skull was old, the color of parchment. There was a black scorch mark around a ragged hole near the temple.

Julie thought it looked a lot like a bullet hole.

"Who is this guy?", Tara asked.

Ozzy peered nervously around the doorframe to find Tara holding a skull in her hands.

"Whoa!" Ozzy said. "Is that real? Can I see?"

The boy shouldered past his mother and reached for the skull still clutched in Tara's hands.

"No." Julie snapped, and felt her headache return with a vengeance carving a line between her eyebrows.

"Tara, put it back." She said, and grabbed Ozzy's shoulder, pulling him back. "And close that case."

Tara could tell from her mother's tone that there was no wriggle room here and she did what she said.

"And you." Julie said to Ozzy. "Go find a book and

read on the couch."

"What about the keys and the phone?" Ozzy asked.

"I'll keep looking." She told him. "You two...you've helped enough. Go take a break."

Julie waited until Tara had relocked the case of skulls and then left the spare bedroom pushing her brother ahead of her down the hall. Once they were gone Julie swept her light over the green metal gun case at the back of the room. She hoped her kids didn't notice it. She took a couple steps closer and saw that the door had been left open and that weapons and ammunition lay inside. Quietly she closed the metal door.

Julie backed out of the small room and secured the door behind her as she heard Ozzy call out, "Dad's back."

JULIE SAW the look on her husband's face as he stepped inside the cabin and it stopped her in her tracks. She had been with Nick since high school and over the years they had begun to develop what amounted to a low level telepathy between the two of them. She could read his face like a book, even with the ice crusting his eyebrows.

His face was the color of skim milk, save for the red tip of his nose and the tops of his cheeks. When his eyes met hers she could feel her hands begin to shake at her sides. She had only seen him that scared once before: when Ozzy had been hit by a car riding his bike in front their house.

Ozzy and Tara were sitting on the couch again, but

when they saw their dad's face they swivelled in their seats and whatever questions they had, died in their throats.

"What's wrong?" Julie asked.

Nick shook his head, ignoring her question.

"Get your coat on. I need to show you something."

"What is it?" Julie whispered, but Nick just shook his head.

"You find the keys?"

"No." Julie told him. "What's wrong?"

"Nothing. Nothing's wrong." He said. "Just...keep looking for them, okay guys?" And then to Julie. "You have to come with me."

"Dad, tell us what's going on?" Tara finally asked.

"Just stay in the cabin, okay?" Nick told them. "Just stay here by the fire. We'll be right back."

Julie pulled on her coat that was still damp and then dragged on her cold and wet gloves and hat and joined Nick at the door.

Nick switched on the UV flashlight and nodded to Julie, as he opened the cabin door and ushered them both into the storm.

Tara and Ozzy wasted no time and ran to the rear of the cabin and watched from the back bedroom window as their parents moved slowly through the snow, past the buried truck.

Their father lead their mother by the hand down a path between looming pine trees, the glow of his purple flashlight swinging wildly left and right scanning for threats.

"Where the hell are they going?" Tara asked, her breath clouding the frigid glass.

Ozzy had no answers.

He stood on his tip toes next to his sister, barely breathing as he watched the purple light flicker and fade as his parents disappeared into the darkness.

~

"WHAT IS IT? WHAT'S WRONG?" Julie said as Nick dragged her along, shuffling and stumbling through the snow.

"Just...wait." He said, his light flicking nervously left and right across the path.

"*Nick*." She said finally, and yanked her arm out of his grasp. "What the hell? Where are you taking me?"

Nick stopped and double backed to where his wife stood glaring at him. Again he swept his UV flashlight over the wall of pines that swayed and crowded around them, drawing closer.

"I found something." He said, just above a whisper. "In the shed."

"What shed? Why are you whispering?" She asked peering further down the snowy path seeing nothing but shifting tree branches and swirling snow.

"It's there." He said quietly. "Hidden against the rock face."

"Nick. There's something wrong here." She said. "Whoever this guy is he has a case full of skulls in there."

"What?"

135

Julie nodded. "Skulls, Nick." She repeated. "We need to leave."

"You have no idea." Nick replied. "But you have to see this. I don't know what else to do."

Julie stared down the empty path and then found Nick's eyes. She nodded and he took her hand. Together they walked to the end of the path though the trees, Nick's purple light leading the way until the bunker came into view.

Just the sight of it gave Julie a cold feeling in the pit of her stomach.

Nick hurried to the metal door and wrenched it open wide enough for them to slip inside.

"What's in there?"

Julie had stopped in the snow a few feet behind him. Her face as pale as the flakes falling around her.

Nick wanted to tell her, to warn her, but he needed her help. He couldn't allow her to freak out and spin away.

"Nick." She said, taking a small step backward toward the cabin. "You fucking tell me right now what's in there."

"You have to see." Nick said, reaching for her hand, but this time she skittered away, out of reach.

"No." She said. *"Now."*

Nick seemed to deflate. His shoulders rolled forward and he looked, smaller. Older.

"There's a woman in there." He said finally.

"What?"

"In a cage..." Nick told her. "I think she's dead."

136

TWENTY-FIVE

N ick covered his mouth with his glove as he crept inside, disappearing around the doorframe. Julie stayed a few feet back, hesitating at the doorway, her hands bracing her against the doorframe. Her body seemingly unwilling to let her enter this place.

Standing there at the edge of the darkness she felt the warmth of the fetid air press against her skin. The stench of vomit and shit reminded her of a hospital ward and her stomach did a slow forward roll.

Slowly, she edged inside and then hurried to stay close to Nick. She saw his strange purple light sweep over a desk topped with computer terminals and screens. No lights flickered and both screens were dark and furred with frost. A metal gun case identical to the one she spotted in the cabin stood in the corner, its door left opened as well.

"What is this place?" She whispered.

"Just look."

Julie followed Nick deeper into the shed and closer to the smell of human decay. Her husband shined his light over the far end of the room where a metal cage ten feet by ten feet was bolted to the concrete floor and affixed to the rock wall behind it.

"What the hell..."

The woman lay curled in a fetal position atop a collapsible army cot. She faced the rock wall with her arms pillowed beneath her head, her legs pulled up to her chest. The woman's greasy black hair spilled over the edge of the makeshift bed, nearly reaching the floor.

She wore a plain cotton dress that was streaked with dried blood and what could have been mud. The fabric was pulled tight against her side and the sharp edges of the woman's ribs were clearly visible through the material. The skin of her legs was the color of wet cement and mottled with painful looking bruises and marbled with spidery black veins.

Julie drew closer to the rusty bars of the cell, studying the woman for any signs of life.

"Julie." Nick said, holding out his hand, warning her to stay back from the cell, but she ignored him. She was a nurse and had been for nearly fifteen years. It was in her nature to help those that were ill and in pain.

"I can't tell if she's breathing." Julie told him.

"I know." Nick said. "Who knows how long she's been in here."

Julie moved to the door of the cell and pulled on the

handle. The door was locked and the metal door rattled and clanked in its frame.

"I have to get in there." She told Nick, but again, he held up his hand.

"What?" She asked. "I have to see if she's breathing."

"Wait, okay. Just wait....*look.*" Nick said and slowly played the beam of the UV flashlight over the soles woman's bare feet. Immediately the skin caked with grime and mud began to darken. The skin actually smouldered and cracked. Tiny tendrils of smoke spiralled up from the woman's flesh.

The top layer of her skin curled and peeled away from her foot like so much birch bark in a bonfire. The woman shifted weakly in place, dragging her blistered foot away from the light, whimpering.

"What the hell are you doing?" Julie snapped. "You're hurting her."

Immediately Nick moved the light away from the woman's body and again the woman grew still. Motionless.

"I wanted to show you."

"You coulda just told me."

"You wouldn't have believed me." He said.

Julie pressed up against the bars and angled her own light into the cell playing her beam over the woman's feet. The skin was still black and charred and looked very tender, but the reaction to the light was over. Whatever it was.

"But still, seriously, what the hell is that? She's allergic to UV light? To sunlight?"

"It's something like that Nick. *Jesus*. Don't do that again. We gotta find some keys or some way to open this door. Get her out of here."

"But...seriously, Julie...have you seen that before? Ever?"

Julie didn't answer. She dragged her cell phone from her jeans pocket and activated her flashlight. With the small cone of white light she searched the floor and then moved to the computer desk and started opening drawers.

Nick stepped closer to the bars, moving around to the far side. From this angle he could see a small curl of white vapor escaping her cracked lips. Her lips were moving. She was whispering something. Nick edged closer to the bars, but he still couldn't pick it out.

A jingle of keys gave him a jolt and he staggered back from the cell.

Julie strode to the cage door, a ring of keys in her gloved fist. Sudden terror spiked through Nick's bloodstream.

"Don't open that." He said, cutting his wife off before she reached the cell door.

"What? Why?"

"Where are we going to take her?"

"At least to the cabin." Julie said, dodging around her husband and reaching the cell.

"And then what?" Nick wanted to know.

"I'm not leaving her in this fucking cell, Nick." Julie snapped. "What if it was Tara? We need to help her. She'll die out here. It's a miracle she isn't dead already."

Julie selected the first key on the ring and jabbed it into the lock. The key didn't turn and Nick found himself wishing the key would snap off, trapping the woman inside her cell forever.

"This is a mistake, Julie." He said, as she tried the next key. "There's something wrong with her. The light."

A sudden thought flared like neon across his brain and he blurted it out without thinking.

"What if she's locked in there for a reason?"

Julie eyed him, her face twisting with a new expression that bordered on disgust, and then she tried the second key on the ring.

"How are you going to live with yourself if she dies? Whatever is wrong with her, she's not a monster, Nick. Whoever locked her in this cell is the monster."

The second key didn't turn either. She yanked it from the mechanism and stuck the final one into the lock.

The last key twisted easily and Nick listened to the tumblers fall into place. Julie grabbed the handle of the cell door and with a squeal of rusted hinges the door swung wide.

Nick spied a disgusting bowl on the floor that held a pile of what looked like a chunk of wet dog food. The food looked untouched and had grown a fringe of mold. Next to that there was an empty water bowl that wasn't filled with water. It looked like dried blood.

In two strides Julie was standing beside the bed and using her flashlight to study every inch of the filthy woman.

Nick stayed by the cell door, his light angled on the

opposite end of the bunker where a tunnel entrance braced by heavy timbers stood clogged with fallen rocks. His light sparked off of a twist of new metal between the boulders. Something was here. Something recent. Until...

A cave in. He thought.

"Oh my God." Julie hissed. "Nick. Get over here."

"What?"

"Come in here." Julie told him. "Hold my light."

Nick did as he was instructed and stepped into the cell where the stink was a million times worse. Julie handed him her phone as she rolled the woman over onto her back.

Nick played the white light over the woman's emaciated breasts and the bulge of her sickly distended belly.

"Holy shit." Nick whispered.

"She's pregnant." Julie said. "Or at least...*was.*"

Julie removed her glove and swept away the tangle of the woman's black hair revealing the face beneath. The edges of her cheekbones and the bridge of her nose were thin blades against her papery skin. Julie pressed two fingers to the woman's throat and felt a thin, reedy pulse.

"We have to get her to the cabin. We have to get her warm."

Nick opened his mouth to say something but stopped. Something stopped him. A noise. Somewhere close.

Scratching?

"What is that?" Nick said before Julie shushed him.

Listening.

Scratching. Definitely scratching.

142

Nick picked up the sound and aimed his flashlight toward the tunnel entrance. Rocks and boulders of all sizes blocked the tunnel entrance. The sound continued.

Scratching. Grinding. Grunting.

Was something moving in the rock pile?

"Nick?" Julie whispered. "What is it?"

He waved at her to be quiet, but it didn't work. The sound of her voice echoing off stone, even at a whisper, sounded like gunfire in the tight space.

Nick played his own purple light over a tiny one foot gap between the collapsed tunnel ceiling and the rubble below, zeroing in on the sound of movement. But it was gone.

It was nothing.

"Help me get her up." Julie said, tugging on Nick's sleeve. "We gotta go."

Nick stood staring down at the painfully thin woman.

"We're going to have to carry her." She told him.

Thick black veins stood out against the woman's alabaster skin, creeping across the flesh of her face and arms like voracious vines.

"Are you ready?" Julie asked. Again Nick nodded and carefully reached under the woman's neck and behind her knees. In one smooth motion he lifted her off of the bed with a groan, as his back twinged with the effort.

"Are you okay?" Julie asked him. "Is she heavy?"

Nick shook his head and grimaced. It wasn't the weight. It was the smell. The woman stank and not with just body odor or feces, but something else. It made Nick think of turmeric, but that wasn't it. It was a spice that he couldn't place. The smell of it hit him in the back of the throat.

Julie took the UV flashlight from Nick and moved to the front door of the bunker. Nick followed and stared down at the woman's face. Her rice paper eyelids were closed but Nick could see her eyeballs knocking wildly back and forth as if caught in a fever dream.

Julie pushed open the bunker door and a face full of swirling snow and ice were there to meet her. She turned away, pulling her scarf up higher on her face before shining the light on Nick who was five feet behind her staring at the tunnel choked with boulders.

"Are you ready?"

TWENTY-SIX

O zzy and Tara stood by the window of the cabin overlooking the porch and the driveway beyond as their parents, bundled up against the cold, shuffled through the snow. Quickly disappearing into the dark.

"Where are they going?" Ozzy asked, as they watched the large cone of their father's purple flashlight shrink to nothing. Tara didn't answer.

"What's out there?"

Ozzy stared at his older sister, staring silently into the storm, her face close enough to the window to frost the glass.

"Tara?"

Ozzy's shrill, scared little voice seemed to snap his sister out of her trance. Tara blinked and then she fixed her green eyes on him.

She said finally. "We need to find those truck keys. Or a phone."

"But we looked everywhere already."

"So, we're gonna look again." She told him. "We have to leave, Ozzy."

Tara nudged him toward the kitchen.

"Start in there. I'll check the back rooms again. And stay away from that goddamn bookshelf."

"I'm gonna tell mom you swore." Ozzy told her, but his heart wasn't in it and his sister just rolled her eyes as she spun away down the hall.

"This is bullshit." He whispered under his breath as he pulled open the first kitchen drawer. He found a notepad, a bunch of pens and spare door handles. Satisfied there were no car keys hiding inside, he moved onto the next one.

Such bullshit.

Tara was losing her shit. Her anxiety had been redlining for most of the day but now she was beginning to shake. It started with her foot and knee, jumping up and down like a spring but now it had graduated to her hands. The cabin had begun to feel like it was closing in on her. Crushing her.

She needed to find a way out of here.

She started in the master bedroom. She tore open drawers and rummaged through them with a vengeance. Spare change, a deck of cards held together with a rubber band, empty packs of cigarettes and a couple of old disposable lighters. But no keys. She checked the clothes draped over the chair and patted down the bedsheets, hoping not to feel anything wet, *God help her*.

"Anything yet?" she called out to her brother. Thinking that if he's not actually searching like she was, he would have a serious beat down coming.

"Nothing." He called back, suddenly appearing at the doorway of the master bedroom.

"What if he took his phone and car keys with him?" He asked.

"Why are you not searching?"

"I checked everywhere." He told her.

"Check again, moron." She said. "They have to be here."

When they heard the jangling, discordant notes, they froze. Ozzy opened his mouth to say something but Tara waved a hand at his face so fast he bit back his words.

"Shut up." She mouthed.

Ringing...

They heard ringing.

It was a phone.

Holy shit.

The phone rang again and Tara nearly bowled over her baby brother over rushing toward the weak trilling sound of the phone.

The pair stepped into the hall and then straight into the opposite spare bedroom where the boxes of food and plastic crates were stacked.

"Where is it coming from?" Ozzy said as the phone stopped ringing.

"Shit!" Tara said. "Please. *Please*."

Ozzy opened a nearby crate and pawed through the dry cereal packets finding nothing but food.

And then thankfully, the ringing started again.

It wasn't coming from the spare bedroom. Tara listened closely, her eyes closed, concentrating. She drifted back out into the hall and the ringing got louder.

She stepped into the bathroom and pulled open drawers finding toothbrushes and toothpaste, a finger-nail clipper and a small first aid kit.

But no phone.

Finally, she ripped open the lower cupboard doors and heard the ringing coming from a small gray plastic box wedged back against the wall.

Tara snatched the tiny case out of the gloom and slammed it on the bathroom counter. The case was hard plastic and she needed to unlock two clasps. Nestled inside a bed of styrofoam was a bulky bright yellow cellular phone that looked more like an expensive walkie-talkie.

And it was ringing.

"Answer it." Ozzy said. "Do it!"

Tara snatched the walkie talkie looking device out of the styrofoam and turned it over in her hands searching the array of buttons adorning the front.

"How do you work this?"

Ozzy snatched the phone from his older sister and pushed the green button on the front. Suddenly an older man's voice came through the speaker.

"Jesus, are you there? Harry? I was about to give up on you." The man said. "I thought you died on me, man. I need the new manuscript by next week or Random House will send someone to break my kneecaps. I'm not fucking around here. I know you said you need more time, but at least give me something. *Anything...*"

Ozzy held the satellite phone at arm's length looking as though it might bite him.

"Say something." Tara hissed.

"Harry, are you there?" The man asked, sounding annoyed.

Finally, Ozzy said, "Hello?"

"Who the fuck is this?" The man asked.

"Who's *this*?" Ozzy countered.

"Kid, this isn't funny. Put Harry on the line." The man said.

"Uh...he's not here right now, but--"

"Then how'd you get his phone? What the fuck is going on? Where's Harry?"

Ozzy opened his mouth to say something, anything, but the man, whoever he was, beat him to the punch.

"Professor Marks. Ring a bell? Put him on the phone. Now. I'm serious."

Ozzy was fading. He stared up at his sister, pleading.

Finally, Tara snatched the chunky satellite phone from his sweaty grip.

"My name is Tara Jackson and my family and me were in a car crash. We found this cabin and we need help. We don't know where the professor is, but you need to call the police or the mountain rangers or whatever the hell 'cause we need help."

There was a pause and what sounded like a sigh, and then the man was back on the line.

"Kid. I don't know who you are but I'm not fucking around here. That phone is not a toy. If this is a joke it's not funny."

"This isn't a joke." Tara said. "Our car went off the road."

"Where are your parents?" The man said, cutting her off. "Where's Harry?"

"They're outside." She said.

"Harry's outside? Outside where?"

"I don't know where Harry is. We need help. Please. Just send--"

"Tell Harry I need to speak with him and I don't fucking appreciate being dodged like this. If he needs more time that's one thing, but this is bullshit. Tell him to call his agent pronto. If not sooner. You tell him that. Okay kid?"

Tara clutched the device in her hands so hard the plastic creaked, anger and frustration bubbling over.

"Please, listen. We need help. We don't even know where we are. We--"

Suddenly a *beep...beep...beep* began blaring from the phone.

"What the hell is this?" Tara said, holding out the phone to Ozzy. "What's that noise?"

Ozzy studied the display and saw a battery icon was flashing.

"Kid? Kid?" The man kept repeating. "Somebody talk to me."

"It's the battery." Ozzy told her.

Tara snatched the phone back from Ozzy just as the display went dark.

Dead.

"*Noooo!*" Tara moaned. "Hello? Hello!"

She stabbed the buttons on the front of the phone in a panic, but the dark display didn't change.

"It's dead, Tara."

"Fuck!" Tara said and raised the phone over her head like she was going to throw it through the wall.

"Don't!" Ozzy yelled, holding up his hands. "Wait."

Tara felt hot tears burning her eyes and she collapsed to the floor against the bathroom cabinet. She pulled her knees up to her chest, wrapped her arms around herself, rested her face on her forearms and cried.

She didn't care about the curly silver hairs on the hardwood, she didn't care about the mold in the sink. She just wanted to go home.

Ozzy sat down quietly in front of her, his tiny hands nervously turning the device over and over again as his sister cried into her sleeve.

"You think he'll call someone?" He whispered.

TWENTY-SEVEN

T ara and Ozzy drifted down the hall and into the main living area. Ozzy still clutched the dead satellite phone when movement through the frosted windows caught their eye.

They stepped closer and pressed their faces to the freezing glass. Snow continued to swirl out of the dark, passing a thin veil over the image of their parents. The sheet of snow broke away and Tara saw her mother and father, shuffling slowly through the storm, their heads bent close together as if they were holding each other up. But no, there was something else. Something between them.

"What is that?" Ozzy whispered.

Through the windows the kids watched as their parents stopped suddenly, and adjusted their grip on...

"Is that a...*girl?*" Ozzy said.

∼

THE WOMAN WAS HEAVIER than she looked, and thirty feet away from the cabin Julie and Nick were gassed. Nick had the woman under the arms, while Julie carried the woman's ankles in each hand as together they awkwardly navigated through the knee high snow.

Nick stepped into a hole and fell to his knees dropping his end of the pregnant girl into the snow. She didn't seem to mind. If she moaned or made a sound the wind stole it away before he could hear it.

Nick cursed under his breath, and found he didn't even have the wind to curse. Greasy sweat trickled down his back between his shoulder blades. He focused on his breathing.

"We have to get her inside." Julie told him.

He knew that. He nodded. That was still the plan. Unless he died of a heart attack first.

When he could draw a breath without wheezing Nick muttered, "Sorry."

He reached down and scooped up the woman. Julie saw what he was going for and helped position her on his shoulder.

"Are you okay?" She asked.

Again Nick nodded, feeling anything but okay. He looked up and saw the kids in the window watching them. What were they going to tell them?

"Ready?"

Nick took a step toward the cabin and then another. Soon he was at the wooden porch. While gripping the railing, he was able to lean on Julie enough to offset the weight of the woman as they climbed the three steps.

"Open the door!" Nick shouted to the kids. "Now!"

The cabin door opened and Tara stood there gawping at her parents. Ozzy peered nervously around his sister's shoulder, his face the color of spoiled milk.

"Who is that?" Tara asked.

"Move!" was all Nick said. Tara flinched as if her father had hit her with a whip and she scampered out of the way, dragging Ozzy with her, deeper into the safety of the kitchen.

Nick and Julie barged past their children, the woman draped over Nick's shoulder and Julie doing her best to support at least some of the weight.

"Mom, what's wrong with her?" Tara asked, but her mother ignored her.

Tara and Ozzy edged away deeper into the kitchen when the stink of the woman finally hit them. A fetid stew of feces and body odor and something else. Something sickly sweet like the smell of rotting meat.

Tara held her sleeve over her mouth to stop herself from dry heaving as she closed the cabin door and set the deadbolt.

The children watched silently as their parents hurried down the narrow hall and disappeared into the master bedroom. The door slamming closed behind them a moment later.

NICK'S KNEES hit the side of the bed and then as gently as he could, he set the pregnant woman down.

Everything ached. Nick's neck felt wrenched out of place, not to mention his lower back. A dull ache radiated outward in every direction.

Julie sprang into action, racing around to the opposite side of the bed, hooking her hands under the woman's right arm.

"Help me shift her higher up on the bed."

Nick sucked in a quick breath, wincing with every movement. He took up his position on the right side of the bed, grabbed the woman's filthy arm and on the count of three, pulled her into place.

With a pillow cradling the woman's head Julie sat next to her on the mattress and checked her pulse, pressing two fingers into the woman's thin throat.

Papery skin, hollow cheeks, the woman's eyes rolled wildly under bruised lids. It was impossible to gauge her age under the dirt and dried blood. Her gray skin was dry and cracked like the desert floor. Deep fissures opened around the edges of her wide mouth and at the corners of her sunken eyes.

Nick guessed she was somewhere in her forties, but he wouldn't have bet on it.

Julie leaned closer to the woman's face, her ear an inch away from the woman's ruined lips. A dry crackle passed as her breathing.

"I can barely feel a pulse." Julie said.

Next Julie lifted the dirty shift the woman wore and examined her swollen stomach. The bulge that had once held a growing child was withered and dark, like rotten fruit. Thick vines of black veins cross-crossed her mottled skin. Julie gently laid her fingers on the woman's distended belly and slowly probed the area, feeling for landmarks and listening.

Nick watched his wife's face slowly crumple inward, like a hand closing into a fist. Angry tears rolled down her cheeks and fell into the twisted sheets.

She shook her head, swiping at the tears.

"I can't feel any movement." She whispered. "I think..."

"Julie." Nick said, edging closer to his wife.

"What?"

"Honey, look at me."

Julie finally did and saw the exhaustion and fear carved into her husband's face. He looked to have aged ten years in the last six hours.

"We can't help her, Julie. We have to leave. Right now."

"I heard you." She said quickly. "But unless you plan on walking off this mountain in the dark we have to find those truck keys. Did anyone check the truck? Living up here all alone. Miles away from anything maybe he left them in the ignition."

Nick hadn't thought of that. No one left keys in their vehicle, let alone in the ignition. But it was worth a shot.

"Okay. I'll look."

Julie nodded and pulled down the woman's peasant dress, covering her stomach. She rose from the bed and found a comforter that had been tossed to the floor. In a practiced movement she spread it evenly over the woman's skeletal frame, tucking the blanket around her, all the way to her chin.

"I need to get her something to drink." Julie said.

TWENTY-EIGHT

N ick stepped into the hall and found Tara and Ozzy waiting for him. Tara had one arm protectively draped over her brother's shoulder, something he hadn't seen in years.

Carefully, Nick eased the door closed behind him, cutting off his children's view of the mystery woman.

"Who is that, Dad?" Tara asked. "Where did she come from?"

Nick ushered his kids back down the hall as they peppered him with questions.

"What's wrong with her?" Ozzy asked. "Is she gonna die?"

Nick made it back into the kitchen and opened the fridge.

"Do we have any juice?"

"Dad." Tara said. A statement. Not a question. "What is going on?"

Nick reached behind a six pack of Michelob and found a half full bottle of Sunny D.

"I don't know who she is, okay?" Nick told them. "She was in the shed out back."

He opened cabinet after cabinet until he found the right one. He selected a chipped Star Wars juice glass and tipped in some juice. He focused on his grip and steadied his shaking hand as best he could, filling the glass to the halfway point.

"A shed? What was she doing out there?" Ozzy asked.

"Your mom thinks she's really sick." Nick said. "When we get out of here, we are gonna take her with us, to the hospital."

"But who is she?" Tara said.

"Yeah, why is she all dirty? She stinks so bad, Dad."

"I don't fucking know." Nick snapped. The kids jolted in place, staring at their father. They noticed now upon closer inspection that his grimy hands were shaking and the loose skin of his face had turned the color of dirty snow. Smudges of purple ringed his eyes.

Nick took a breath as the kids shuffled from foot to foot in front of him. Afraid to speak. Afraid to move.

"I'm sorry." He said quickly. "I'm sorry. I just...I don't know. I didn't mean to yell. It's not your fault."

Nick found a somewhat clean dishrag on the counter and pushed off.

"We found a phone." Ozzy blurted, having forgotten that he was still holding the chunk of plastic in his sweaty grip.

Nick stopped.

"It rang, but it's out of battery." Tara told him. "It needs to be charged."

Nick set the glass of juice and the rag on the counter and took the phone from Ozzy, studying the dark display and the array of buttons.

"What do you mean it rang?"

"The professor kept the thing in a box, under the bathroom sink." Ozzy told him. "I don't think he ever planned on using it."

"We heard it ringing." Tara continued and we answered it.

Nick waited, searching their faces...

"And?" He asked finally.

"He said he wanted to talk to Harry. He said he was his agent or his editor. I can't remember." Ozzy said.

"What did you say?" Nick blurted. "Did you tell him we needed help?"

The two kids nodded emphatically.

"Of course we did." Tara said.

"Well, what did he say? Was he sending someone?"

Tara's eyes flicked to Ozzy who couldn't meet his father's gaze.

"What?" Nick asked. "What did he say?"

"I don't think he believed us." Tara told him.

Nick squeezed the satellite phone as tight as he could, hoping to possibly charge the device with his frustration, before setting it down on the cluttered countertop.

"What about the keys?" Nick asked them. "Any luck?"

The kids shook their heads.

Of course.

He nodded and collected his cup of Sunny D and headed back to the master bedroom.

"Keep looking, okay?" Nick said. "And grab some more firewood. Looks like the fire is getting low."

"Outside?" Tara asked.

"Yeah." He told her. "Around the back of the cabin, against the wall, it's under a tarp. Both of you go. Bring back as much as you can carry. Get some heat in here."

He left them standing there without another word and trudged to the master bedroom door and slipped inside.

Julie was still sitting where he left her, next to the woman. Her ragged breathing sounded like the weak crinkle of cellophane in the quiet room.

"Any change?" Nick asked.

Julie shook her head and accepted the cup of juice and the wash cloth.

"I'm going to see if I can get her to drink anything." Julie told him. "She's so dehydrated. Any luck with the keys?"

"No. But the kids found a satellite phone." Nick said. "They spoke to some friend of the professor, but it sounded like the guy thought he was being pranked."

Julie's expression didn't change from tired acceptance. She nodded and tipped some of the juice into a fresh corner of the rag.

"I'm going to check the truck like you said." He told her. "You never know."

Without another word Julie turned her attention to

her patient. She scooted closer so she could reach the woman's lips with the tip of the cloth and squeezed a thin drizzle of the sugary yellow drink into her mouth.

Nick watched for a few seconds as the woman's lips mechanically closed and rubbed together, accepting the gift. In the near dark he saw her rough tongue peek out of the shadow of her mouth, searching for more. The tip of her tongue looked sharp.

It looked like a weapon.

TWENTY-NINE

Bundled up against the elements Tara and Ozzy marched, as ordered, out of the cabin and down the porch to the covered wood pile.

Tara pulled back the moldy tarp revealing the stack of firewood and began loading her brother's waiting arms to capacity. She could barely see his eyes between the lowest edge of his toque and layer of scarf that covered the bottom half of his face. But she could tell he didn't look well. He looked scared.

He was carrying three large chunks of maple, or whatever the hell kind of wood it was, when his arms began to tremble. Tara selected a final, smaller piece for his load and set it gently on top.

"Go ahead." She told him. "I'll be right there."

He didn't move though. He stood firm.

"You can't carry anymore, idiot." She said. "You're already shaking."

"I want to wait for you." He said, his voice muffled by the scarf.

Tara didn't make fun of him. Didn't chide him for being a pussy, as was her usual M.O., she simply nodded and secretly thanked him, as she didn't want to be out here all alone either.

Quickly, she gathered up as much as she could carry, sharp splinters of the wood digging into her new ski jacket, and headed back to the cabin door.

NICK OPENED the cabin door and once again stepped into the storm. It didn't get any easier, but at least he was not surprised when the first strong gust of icy wind stole his breath away.

To his right his children stomped through the snow covered porch, their arms loaded with wood. He opened the door for them as they slipped inside, poor Ozzy's shoulders shaking with the effort.

As soon as they crossed the threshold he hauled the door closed and made his way down the porch steps to the truck.

He yanked on the passenger side door. Locked.

"Shit." He spat. "Of course it's locked."

He cleared away the snow covering the passenger window and stared through to the driver's side door and saw that the manual pull knob of the lock was raised.

Nick raced through the snow to the driver's side and pulled open the door. He had to work the door open and closed a few times using the bottom edge as a plow in order to clear enough snow to get inside, but he finally squeezed his body through the gap and dropped into the torn cloth driver's seat. The rusty springs groaned beneath his weight.

His hands went to the ignition and found the keys were missing. He couldn't have been that lucky. He checked the visors on both sides, the glove box, the center console. He even checked under the seats.

No keys.

Nick wanted to scream. To shout. To do something that made him feel remotely useful. He had gotten such a boost after finding the cabin. He had done it. He had found his family shelter and heat and some sustenance. He was a hero. But almost immediately he realized that they were trapped. He needed to find a way out. A solution. He stared out at the partially covered windshield.

Black trees bent and swayed in the wind. Drifts of snow like razored lace swept across the moonlit landscape.

They had shelter and heat and some food at least. It wasn't much, but they wouldn't starve. And the storm couldn't last forever. Soon it would clear and he would form a plan. Maybe they, or he, would have to hike down the mountain. Follow the road and hope to reach someone with a phone. Or a working vehicle.

Nick's breath formed ragged clouds in the truck and he realized he had started shaking again. He needed to get back inside.

He reached for the door handle when a roar erupted

from the darkness. Angry and hungry and deep as rolling thunder.

His hand froze in place, his fingers curled over the release lever.

The sound rumbled over the wind and everything stopped. Nick even stopped breathing and if asked, he would have bet that, at least for a few seconds, his heart stopped beating as well.

His mind struggled to assign the sound to an animal and failed. Was it a wolf? No. A bear? Possibly.

He stared out through the windshield, into the dark and waited. It didn't take long. Another roar clawed its way from the blackness beyond the twisting trees. It was coming from the bunker.

Nick was sure of it. It was coming from the bunker and it definitely wasn't a bear.

Fear crippled his senses and paralyzed his limbs. He heard himself whispering a single word over and over and over again just below a whisper...

'...move...move...move...'

He risked another glance through the windscreen and seeing nothing there but the swirling dark he yanked on the door handle and shouldered open the door. The metal hinges creaked in protest, but he managed to slither through the opening. He kept his eyes edged toward the path through the trees and the bunker beyond, cloaked in black.

He eased the truck door closed and then he was off. His heart kicked into a gear he didn't know he had and suddenly his feet were slamming down through the snow drifts like pistons as panic electrified every muscle fibre.

Nick leapt up the three steps in a single bound, stumbled at the top, and fell to his hands and knees. Gasping, he struggled to his feet and nearly fell through the cabin door, slamming it hard enough behind him to rattle the wall.

Behind him Tara and Ozzy had fed more wood into the fire and now the flames were licking at the top of the hearth. They stared in horror at their father as he burst through the door, shaking and panting.

"Did you hear that?" Ozzy asked, knowing the answer before the words left his mouth. "Was it a bear?"

Nick's eyes flicked over the scared faces of his children and turned back to the door. With a shaking hand he snapped the dead bolt into place and waited, his breath held, burning in his lungs, his eyes pinned to the windows and the blizzard beyond.

Waiting.

CHAPTER

THIRTY

J ulie heard what sounded like thunder roll through
the darkness outside and tilted her head toward
the window. In the silence that followed the wind
threw handfuls of tiny ice shards at the window
glass, rattling the frame in the wall.

She thought what she heard was thunder, but when
it came again she knew she was wrong. Thunder boomed
and rumbled. This was something different. Something
personal. This was angry and low to the ground. A deep,
guttural howl.

Beside her in the bed the woman moaned and shifted
in her sleep. Julie turned her attention to her patient and
pressed the cloth soaked in orange drink to the woman's
lips.

She wasn't sure if it was the dark or the dirt, but the
cleaned area around the woman's mouth looked very
different in the light of the bedroom lantern.

Julie added more liquid to the rag and the woman

sucked on the end of the cloth like a starved newborn. As Julie watched the wrinkles around the corner of the woman's mouth had begun smooth. Perhaps the lines looked worse, filled in with dirt and grime inside the harsh light of the bunker, but whatever had happened it had improved the woman's appearance tenfold.

As Julie squeezed more liquid into her waiting mouth the woman's sharp, dry tongue darts out greedy for more.

My god...

The woman's tongue looked more than dry. It had the texture and color of tree bark with a sharpened end. Its pointed tip darted out, impossibly long, between the woman's lips that had bloomed full and almost pink.

Excited by the sudden transformation Julie grabbed the plastic jug and gently tipped a tiny sip into the woman's open mouth. However the woman wasn't ready for that just yet. She choked on the mouthful and she spat the thick orange liquid up over her chin.

"Shit." Julie whispered. "Sorry. Gettin' ahead of myself there."

Julie grabbed the cloth and mopped the woman's chin, clearing away the trail of sticky juice running down her throat.

The woman's nose was straight and true and her cheeks had filled out a touch as if she had just spent the week eating turkey dinners and not just had a few sips of sugar water. Julie continued to clean around the woman's mouth revealing more and more supple pale flesh.

The woman's papery eyelids slid open.

Something wrong about her eyes.

They were the deepest brown, almost black. But it wasn't that...it was the whites of her eyes. They weren't white at all. A lattice of broken blood vessels had rendered the whites of her eyes entirely bloodshot.

The woman's dark eyes swivelled and focused on Julie's face, the curve of her neck, the line of her jaw.

A deep growl rumbled from the woman's throat.

Her mouth opened and lunged forward as fast as a rattlesnake. The woman's tiny jagged teeth snapped on Julie's right hand that held the wet rag. In that awful second, Julie heard the *clack* of the woman's jaw snapping shut like a bear trap. The bones in Julie's index and middle finger of her right hand broke like toothpicks with a loud splintering crack.

Fear and pain raced through her body like an electric current. She yanked her hand away but she was trapped. The woman growled and her head thrashed from side to side as her ragged teeth sawed through Julie's flesh, and cartilage and bone.

Blood exploded from Julie's hand, hot and bright in the lantern light. She was finally able to throw her body to the left, off the bed. The sound of tearing flesh was followed by a brutal *pop* that filled the space. Julie fell backward to the hardwood floor, the scream in her throat still trapped in her chest until she held her shaking hand to her face and she saw the ruin that remained. Crimson bubbled from her mangled digits and

poured down her wrist as Julie finally found her breath
and unleashed a bloodcurdling scream.

Nick ripped through the front door of the cabin and eyed
his children's ghostly faces. They were frozen in place
mid-argument standing in front of the fireplace, both of
them grabbing the same chunk of oak, their eyes staring
down the darkened hallway.

"Nick! Nick!"

Julie screamed again, a desperate grating scream and
Nick rushed toward the sound.

Nick burst through the door and found the dirty
pregnant woman down on the floor between the bed and
the door. She was on all fours, her jaw working overtime,
chomping on something hard and crunchy. She eyed
Nick with deep black malice, through the screen of her
greasy black hair. A small pool of blood splattered the
floor between her grimy hands.

A voice creaky and hoarse from disuse issued from
the woman's throat. A language of sharp consonants and
curses filled the silence of the room.

"What the fuck?"

The woman spoke a language he couldn't possibly
understand. He scanned the room for his wife but she
wasn't there.

Footsteps behind him rushed to a halt as the kids
piled into the doorframe, desperate to see. To help. Nick

held them back and pushed them down the hallway with one hand.

"Don't." He warned. "Stay there."

Nick saw movement beyond the bed, a puddle of blood glistening in the lantern light.

"Julie?"

Julie climbed to her knees and used the edge of the bed to pull herself up. Her pallor was moonlight. Her eyes looked faraway and unfocused.

"Oh Jesus..." Nick muttered.

Nick took a step into the bedroom and the woman advanced, scuttling forward on all fours, spitting a wad of blood at his feet. Testing him.

Nick waited, debating...

What are you?

The woman's jaw unhinged and her back arched and she screamed. At him. Through him. The sound was guttural and brutal and familiar. Nick could feel it in his chest. He could feel the sound grow and expand, to fill not just the bedroom, but the cabin. He could feel it claw over his skin and dig into his ears. Burrowing into his brain.

He could feel his heart slamming against his ribs, desperate to break free.

Her screaming continued, growing louder and louder and louder...

It had to stop.

He could hear the kids crying in the hall. Whimpering.

"Nick!" Julie screamed, her voice barely breaking the

surface of the woman's thunder.

His body moved on instinct. Without thought. He pushed off from the doorframe and after one long stride he was within striking distance. He watched a thick tendril of blood as it dripped from the woman's chin, and splattered on the floor between her hands.

Without breaking stride he drove his size eleven winter boot into the woman's face. The edge of the hard rubber toe hit her just under the chin and snapped her head back with a loud pool ball crack of upper and lower jaws knocking together, hard enough to leave shards of teeth on the hardwood floor.

The droning sound of her screaming was cut brutally short leaving only the echoes, ghosts of what was, to scatter and fade and die. Silence rushed in.

The woman's body lay crumpled on the floor, a twisted heap.

Nick moved deeper into the bedroom studying the dirty woman moaning softly. Blood bubbled through split lips and broken teeth. The woman's eyes slid open and her shredded top lip curled away revealing jagged incisors. Nick kicked her again, this time she didn't move. She didn't moan.

Tara and Ozzy crowded behind him in the doorway. Still whimpering. Tears spilling over their cheeks. Their hands clutching each other.

"Nick." Julie said weakly from the opposite side of the bed. "Please."

She had slipped down below the edge of the bed

now, sitting on the floor, her ruined hand clutched to her chest.

Nick rushed to her, and dropped to his knees. Crimson blood had painted the front of Julie's sweater and soaked through the material. Nick gently peeled away his wife's hand and inspected the damage. Her two fingers were now nothing more than ragged bleeding stumps. Her hands shook incessantly, but she was doing her best to keep pressure on the wounds.

His stomach clenched and he could taste bile in the back of his throat. He had to look away for fear he might add his own vomit to the mess. He stared at his wife, who stared serenely in his general direction, her milk-white skin, flecked with blood.

A greasy layer of sweat coated his skin. It stung his eyes and froze across his back. He had to do something.

"Oh baby. Julie. Oh Jesus Christ."

"She ate them..." Julie whispered into Nick's face. "She ate them, Nick. My fingers."

He scanned the room and dragged a pillow down off of the bed. He ripped the pillow case away and, after once again uncurling his wife's fingers from the wound, he gently wrapped the yellowed pillow case around her damaged hand.

"It's okay. It's okay." Nick said, casting a glance over his shoulder at the woman lying still.

From where he knelt in front of his wife, he could only see the bottoms of her grimy feet and lower half of her calves. Long black toenails curled out from muddy toes.

"Mom?" Tara's voice was small and wavering from the doorway. "Are you okay?"

Nick lifted his head and found them standing at the threshold, holding the doorframe for balance, for security. They looked so young in the weak light.

"Tara." Nick said. "I need your help, honey."

But Tara was frozen in place, her eyes locked on the pregnant woman. On the pools of blood cooling on the floor.

"Tara! Now! Help me."

Her father's voice snapped and Tara flinched. Her fear temporarily overridden, she hurried inside, leaving Ozzy alone gripping the doorframe.

Tara's face crumbled when she saw her mother. A blood soaked pillow case clutched to her chest, her skin sweaty and pale. Her blonde hair stuck to her cheeks in thick tangles.

"Tara, honey." Nick said. "Look at me. We need to get your mother up and out into the living room, okay?"

Tara nodded, focusing on her father's voice. On his face. He's scared too, she could tell, but he's in motion. He's *doing*.

Tara and Nick moved into position and on three they lifted Julie onto her feet. With Nick in the lead they pivoted toward the door, giving the woman on the floor a wide berth in the narrow confines.

Ozzy watched them come and eased backward through the doorway, down the hall, staying in front and staying with them. He fought desperately not to cry.

CHAPTER

THIRTY-ONE

In the living room Nick and Tara led Julie over to the couch and slowly sit her down on the rumpled cushions. Ozzy prepared a few pillows beneath her head and Julie reclined, her bloody hand still clutched to her chest.

"You have to stop the bleeding." Julie whispered. "You need the first aid kit."

"Find the first aid kit, Tara." Nick said. "It's in mom's bag.'

Already the pillow case was soaked through with blood.

"She was...eating her fingers." Ozzy whispered, mostly to himself. "Why was she eating them?"

Julie's face had taken on the color of old stone. Nick checked her pulse and slowly peeled away the pillow case.

"You have to...stop the bleeding." She said again. "You need the first aid kit."

"Tara, where's the first aid kit?"

"I'm trying." Tara called back. "I can't find it. It's not here."

"Ozzy."

But Ozzy was so scared he couldn't think straight. He barely registered Nick. His eyes pinned to the yellow pillow case and the blood, his mother's blood, and the sound of that strange woman crunching through his mother's bones.

"Tara. Forget that. Get over here."

Tara did what she was told and knelt in front of her mother, tears streaming down her face. She wrapped her hands around her mother's and held tight.

"Keep pressure on her hand. I'll be right back." Nick said. "Just keep pressure on her hand."

NICK OPENED the backpack he'd been carrying from the wreck and dumped the contents onto the floor. Mixed in with the spare clothes and the many cables for their useless devices was his wife's faded red first aid kit.

Back in front of the fire he unzipped the pouch and spread apart the kit so that Julie could see it. It had been years since he had been asked to dress a wound or even apply a bandaid.

"There..." She said, gesturing with her chin. "The bandages."

Nick fumbled through the packages crammed

177

together until his fingers found the right one. Julie nodded.

"Yes." She said. "Careful. Open it..."

Nick gripped the edges of the package with shaking fingers but try as he might, he couldn't tear it. When he finally managed to break the seal the flimsy bandages burst from the package in a fluttering bit of confetti.

"Shit! Shit!"

"It's okay." Julie told him. "It's fine.You gotta place them on...on the...wounds. My fingers. It'll stop the bleeding."

Nick nodded to Tara who stepped aside.

Nick removed the cloth from Julie's hand and slowly placed the first bandage onto the ragged stumps of her fingers.

Julie gritted her teeth, but a scream found its way through regardless.

"Sonofabitch!"

Tara scuttled away from her mother, vomit rising in her throat.

Nick pulled away the bandage, but Julie shook her head, using her good hand to keep his where it was.

"It's okay." She hissed. "Keep going."

Nick found another bandage and added it to what remained of his wife's fingers. When the package was finally empty Nick listened as Julie walked him through the next step.

"Grab the roll of bandage now. The gauze. Put it over the fingers and wrap them in tape. To hold...hold them in place."

Nick fished out a roll of medical tape and with Tara's help, he found the end and then began winding it around her stumps, securing them together. In another minute Nick had wrapped and bandaged his wife's fingers in a messy white lump.

"It's good, honey." She said. "It's fine."

Nick slumped to ground in front of her on the floor entirely spent, as his wife leaned back into the couch, her chest slowly rising and falling.

"Jesus Christ." Nick said. "I mean what the actual fuck?"

"There's some...Percocet, in the bedside table." Julie said, finding Nick's eyes. Nick nodded.

With the worst of it over, Ozzy rushed over and slid into the couch next to his mother, gripping her fiercely. Tears and sobs he'd held in came rushing out and soon he was wailing into his mother's shoulder. Soon Tara joined in, wrapping her arms around her mother as best she could.

"It's okay, guys." She whispered. "It's okay."

It's not okay. Nick thought. *Not fucking okay at all.*

Nick climbed to his feet and stomped back down the hall toward the spare bedroom, but not before he lifted a steak knife from the kitchen counter.

"It's fucking not okay." He muttered to himself.

∾

WITH A QUICK LOOK into the master bedroom to make sure the woman still remained down and out, Nick made his way to the spare bedroom.

He didn't know what he hoped for. Alive? Dead? Either way he lost, but in the end he watched from the doorway as her thin chest rose and fell and knew she was still alive.

In the spare bedroom he opened the plastic bins one at a time until he found the one he was looking for. He withdrew a long coil of orange climbing rope and carried it back to the bedroom.

He couldn't tell if she had moved at all, but she was still on the ground and Nick relaxed a little. He could hear the faint sound of her breathing. More of a wheeze than anything, but it was there.

He used the kitchen knife to cut two six foot sections of rope and tied one to each bedpost. With the ropes in place he bent down toward the unconscious woman. He debated bagging her head or gagging her before he attempted to shift her onto the bed, but eventually decided against it. He didn't want to wake her and the least amount of time he spent touching her or fiddling with gags the better.

In the end he grabbed the woman under the arms and half carried, half dragged her up and across the bed until her head was near the wall. He saw the dark point of her tongue peek out from between her lips, but beyond that she was still dead to the world. She moaned and whispered something that he didn't catch and then was silent again.

Quickly, he tied her right hand and then her left, in a simple but effective square knot to the bedposts and after checking his work, he left her alone.

Blood stained her chin and the front of her dirty shift dress. Her left eye had begun to swell where Nick had kicked her the second time and a wave of guilt swept through him now that the rage had subsided.

Normally Nick was a pacifist. He would never dream of hitting a woman, much less a pregnant woman, but this thing tied to the bed. Was not a woman. He wasn't even entirely sure she was human.

He moved to leave and then paused, staring at her face, lolling back against the headboard. She looked different now.

Younger.

It was as if her cheeks had gained some weight. Not much, a few ounces, but it was noticeable. She almost looked...*young*.

In the bunker he put her a touch over forty, now, she looked to be in her twenties. Early twenties at that.

Nick studied the woman's belly pressed against the edge of her dress. Rising and falling and rising...and soon realized that her belly wasn't moving in sync with her breathing. Her belly was moving on its own. Independently.

Something was moving inside her. Nick stared at the woman's filthy skin peeking out beneath the hem of her nightdress. The skin bulged and distorted as something pressed against it from the inside.

A tiny hand, barely discernible imprinted on the woman's flesh.

But there was nothing earlier. No movement. No sounds. Julie was sure.

Nick watched as the tiny hand trailed down the woman's belly, dragging its fingers like needlepoints along her skin.

Those aren't fingers, Nick thought.

"*Holy shit...*"

Nick found the thin blanket left in a swirl at the foot of the bed and draped it over the woman's body, covering her bare stomach and concealing what had begun to claw at her insides.

Those aren't fingers...

Nick switched off the lantern and carried it out of the room, leaving the woman in the dark, moaning softly as he eased the door closed.

Those are claws.

CHAPTER

THIRTY-TWO

t was pleasantly warm in the living room now. Nick had gone out yet again and collected a few more armfuls of wood and the fire crackled and snapped in the hearth as tongues of red and gold licked at the brickwork.

Julie lay on the couch, her back supported by an assortment of pillows and random cushions, Ozzy's small form was cradled around her side. His thin arms encircled his mother's waist, his head pillowed on her chest. Like Julie, he drifted in and out of a shallow sleep. His exhaustion fuelled by flash points of anxiety and fear, while her drowsiness had more to do with the blood loss and the two Percocet Nick had given her from the good professor's side table.

Tara sat next to her mother on the couch in the living room. She monitored her mother's breathing and the pallor of her skin. Her wet stone complexion has brightened some in the heat of the fire. A hint of pink colored her cheeks. Julie's eyes rolled open, bleary and unfocused from the drugs and she offered a weak smile to her daughter. Tara bit her bottom lip to keep the tears from coming.

She knew it was a stupid question but she asked anyways."Are you okay?"

Julie gave her an almost imperceptible nod.

Nick added another log to the already raging fire and watched a cloud of embers swirl up toward the flue. And then he was on his feet. An idea, half formed spurring him to action, it buzzed in his brain like a swarm of fireflies.

Tara was the first to notice.

"What?" She asked. Recognizing the look on his face. The unfocused gaze as the clockwork spun behind his eyes. "Where are you going?"

Without answering his daughter Nick knelt at the end of the couch and slid a palm over his wife's pale cheek. Nick wasn't great with emotion, or showing feeling, or with Valentine's cards or writing poetry. All his compliments would usually come out sounding like sports cliches. But what he was good at was *doing*. He was a fixer and it was killing him to just sit there and do nothing. To be idle.

Julie's voice was raw and she winced from the pain. Her words were brittle things heard just below a whisper.

"Where are you going?" She asked.

"I'm going to check the shed." he said. "The bunker out back."

Julie's eyes, as watery as they were, widened. She shook her head. The line between her brows grew deeper as concern and panic twisted her features.

"It'll be all right." Nick told her. "I'll be right back."

Nick hoped she didn't mention the sound. The animal roar. He wanted to keep going with this plan. He didn't want his wife, or his daughter for that matter, to see how badly his hands were shaking.

Ozzy looked up from where he lay against his mother and said, "No please, Dad. Don't go. Please. What if she wakes up?"

"I'm gonna check the shed again. And we're gonna get out of here. Get mom to a hospital. We can't wait any more."

And without another word Nick was on his feet, his knees popping like pistol cracks in the silence of the cabin.

Tara stood with him. Her hands on her hips, her face set. She looked so much like her mother.

"I'm coming with you."

But Nick was moving. He pulled on his parka and jammed the still damp toque down over his head.

"No honey. You stay here. Look after them."

She didn't fight, instead her eyes flicked down the short hall, to the darkness at the end.

"What about her? What do we do if she wakes up?"

Nick wrapped his scarf around the lower part of his face and grabbed the chunky UV flashlight from the kitchen island where he had left it.

"Nothing." He said. "Don't go in there. Don't even go

near there. She's tied up. She shouldn't be a problem now. Just look after your Mom and Ozzy. I'll be right back."

Tara nodded and their eyes met. Her eyes were red and swollen from crying and she looked like she was tired enough to fall asleep standing up.

"Be right back." He said again and squeezed her shoulder. "Two seconds."

He unlocked the deadbolt and pulled open the door. A torrent of ice and snow lay waiting for this opportunity and swirled inside sweeping a carpet of fresh snow across the hardwood floor. Nick hurried out onto the porch and slammed the door behind him. He heard the deadbolt snap home, locking him out, and immediately his heart ratcheted into a higher gear.

The sharpened wind cut through his blood splattered pants and wet toque, slicing away the warmth he carried with him.

He switched on the purple UV flashlight and swept its beam across the end of the driveway to the slowly disappearing trail of footprints leading through the trees. He stepped off the porch, and into darkness.

SOMETIME LATER OZZY opened his eyes. His mother had fallen asleep, and with his head against her chest, he could hear the wet rattle of her breathing. Slowly, he inched his way backwards along the couch until he could climb over the armrest. He stretched and stared into the dwindling fire. A single log burned in the hearth now. Orange and black it appeared as though it glowed from within on a bed of embers.

He scanned the candlelit room and frowned.

Where is Tara?

A flicker of flame caught his attention and he found his sister, a shadow in the dark as she moved slowly down the hall.

"Where are you going?" Ozzy whispered.

Tara stopped and turned to him, her expression anything but innocent. He recognized that face. It was the same face she wore when Ozzy had noticed the bloody bandages in her bathroom garbage. The bandages that covered her forbidden tattoo.

"Tara. *Don't.*" He said, his voice low, but the threat implied.

"I'm going to the bathroom." She said, creeping further down the hall, her sphere of candlelight lighting her path two feet at a time.

"Put some more wood on the fire."

Ozzy's gaze flicked to the dying fire and he shifted his attention to the wood pile, selecting a few pieces from the stack. When he returned his attention to the hall he could no longer see Tara, or her light.

The flames voraciously crept over the new dry wood finding the weak spots. Knots in the wood cracked and popped and stores of old sap sizzled as the fire grew. Flickering shadows scurried across the floor and climbed over the walls with silent feet.

THIRTY-THREE

T ara crept down the hall, her candle flame flickering and guttering as she moved. The ceaseless wind outside howled and screamed through the gaps in the cabin's construction, forcing the thin walls to shudder.

She didn't plan on using the bathroom but now that she had arrived at the master bedroom door she felt the pressure in her full bladder.

He knew. She thought. He always did. It was like a sixth sense between her and her brother. In a single look he knew if she was full of shit and true to form, he nailed it.

She just wanted to see. She just wanted to ask. *To know.* She had never been so scared, but not knowing what she was. Not understanding this strange wild woman that her father had tied to a bedpost. It irritated her like a splinter in her brain.

Tara eased open the bedroom door and peered inside.

Thankfully the hinges were well greased and the door swung open without a sound.

The bedroom was dark and the candle did very little to help. Tara stepped to the doorway and the meagre light shined on the thin pool of blood near the end of the bed. Something else caught the light. Something small. Tara saw bits of gristle and bone peppered in the blood.

Tara's stomach turned over remembering the crunching sounds as the woman ate her mother's fingers. Loud, bright snaps as if she were chomping her way through a piece of peanut brittle.

The room was silent save for the constant moan and whistle of the wind as it snuck through the window frame. Tara edged inside, just another step, holding the candle out at arm's length. She didn't know what she hoped to gain. What insight she could glean from this savage creature, but the darkness beckoned.

Another step and she could smell the woman now. Heat and humidity, what little there was inside the cabin, had awakened her body. Sweat and old shit, along with the putrid stench of rot, filled the room with a fog. Tara held her free hand to her face, covering her mouth as she took another small step toward the bed.

The amber light curled over the edge of the sheets and spilled over the woman's outstretched legs. Filthy and streaked with old mud and dried blood, her slender calves swept into long broad feet tipped with sharpened toenails so dark yellow they looked black.

Tara raised the candle over the woman's thighs. Her dirty shift dress was hiked up, and had come to rest bunched up just below her swollen belly. Her arms, long and sinewy with muscle hung limply from the ropes her father had tied. But the woman was not asleep.

The woman's curtain of dark hair hid most of her face but her obsidian eyes sparkled like new dimes from behind the screen.

Tara could see that her chin and mouth were stained red with her mother's blood. She stopped moving forward, she set her feet as if expecting a blow, and her weight elicited a creak from the floorboards.

In the dim light of the single candle Tara met the woman's hateful gaze. Sitting by the fire, and then later as she made her way down the darkened hall, she pondered what she was going to ask, what she was going to say, a hundred different questions vying for top rank, but now, at the moment of truth her mind was a void and her mouth was filled with sand.

The wind howled again and rattled the window glass and Tara could feel the woman's glare on her skin like a physical weight. A sound like a hiss, like static on the radio issued from the darkness around the woman's head and with a tiny shift of the light Tara could see that the woman's lips were moving.

Her words were smooth and low and ancient and without understanding a single syllable, Tara knew the woman was definitely not voicing a greeting of peace.

"What are you?"

Tara's whisper cracked in the darkness but the woman's lips stopped instantly, listening.

"Tell me." Tara said again. This time a little stronger, with a little more authority.

The woman's mouth opened again and Tara was shocked to hear her own voice issue from the woman's mouth. It wasn't perfect, but it was close. Very close. Like hearing your own voice on an answering machine. The woman's eyes remained unchanged. Her body so still she could be frozen in amber as she repeated Tara's question, but without the inflection.

"What are you."

"What the fuck?"

"What are you. What are you. What the fuck." The woman parroted Tara's voice relentlessly back at her. "What are you. What are you."

The woman was moving now. Her wrists pulled at the restraints, her long legs folded under her massive belly as she rose to her knees.

"Stop it!" Tara snapped, edging backward now, toward the door, and toward the hall and the safety of the light and the fire.

"Stop it." The woman said in Tara's voice. "Stop it."

"Just shut up! Shut up!" Tara snapped. "Shut the fuck up!"

Suddenly the woman stopped. Her dark eyes flashed on something just beyond Tara. Ozzy stood there, peering around the doorframe. Only a sliver of his pale face was visible in the gloom.

The woman's lips pulled wide in a hungry smile, revealing tiny jagged teeth.

"Ozzy, Jesus." Tara said, spinning toward her brother. "Get out of here."

"What are you doing?" He asked, staring at the woman leaning forward across the bed, her bound arms folding behind her.

"What are you doing?" The woman repeated in Ozzy's panicked voice. "What are you doing?"

Ozzy stared in wonder and horror as this thing spoke to him in his own voice. He was trembling as he backed away, fading into the dark.

"Tara..."

"Come on." Tara said, backpedaling out of the room, ushering Ozzy away from the doorway, away from the woman.

"How does she..." Ozzy whispered as Tara reached for the door, easing it closed.

"Tara..."

Ozzy's voice floating out of the darkened bedroom stopped Tara cold. She raised her candle and stretched out her arm illuminating the shimmering pool of blood and bone, the corner of the bed and the woman, impossibly seated on the edge, her feet somehow planted flat on the floor.

"Tara..."

Ozzy was pulling at Tara's sleeve, pulling her away, but Tara was caught. Frozen in place. Tara reached with the candle until she could see the spill of the woman's tangled hair against her cotton gown. Soft light sparked off of her nearly hidden, glistening eyes.

Tara opened her mouth, a question spilling from her

tongue when the woman threw back her head and roared!

The sound was more animal than human. A ragged, ear-splitting sound that was equal parts rage and desperation. It filled the bedroom like a sudden flood.

The shock wave sent a jolt of electricity through Tara, forcing her to stumble backward. Her hands reached for the wall and she nearly dropped the candle. Hot wax splashed painfully over the back of her hand pulling a wince through gritted teeth.

The woman barked out a laugh and squealed in delight. Foreign words and phrases spilled out of the woman at a breakneck pace as she pulled on her bindings, banging the headboard against the wall. She stood and took a powerful step forward, her pendulous belly swinging low, pressing against the dress as she dragged the entire bed across the floor, the sharp feet of the frame gouging deep grooves in the wood.

Another step and she changed direction, pushing back against the bed, shifting it closer to the far wall. She spun toward the narrow window and once again roared at the rectangle of swirling darkness.

Deep, guttural, desperate screams and suddenly Tara realized what she was doing. She was not just screaming to scare her. She was screaming for help.

She was calling out to someone.

Someone in the dark. Someone like her.

The woman writhed in place, violently twisting and pulling on the ropes binding her in place. Her eyes found Tara again and and this time she screamed, *"Tara!"*

CHAPTER

THIRTY-FOUR

N ick was exhausted and dripping with sweat
when he made it to the bunker door.

He had pushed himself through the knee
high drifts, high stepping at first, leaping from one old
footprint to the next, until he quickly ran out of gas and
returned to slogging through the snow, gouging sloppy
twin tracks through the powdered white.

He leaned against the frozen metal door with his
head pillowed on his forearm, his ragged breath forming
a fog bank around his head that smelled of old coffee and
bile. His poor battered heart slammed painfully against
his ribs and his knees felt as if they had turned to liquid.
He had been shivering cold even inside the cabin and
now, after being repeatedly slashed by the wind, his feet
felt like frozen tingling lumps at the ends of his legs.
Without being a doctor he felt he was in real danger of
slipping wholeheartedly into hypothermia.

He focused on his breathing and after a few moments he heard his heartbeat slow in his ears.

"Okay." He whispered to himself and pulled open the steel door, bulldozing enough drifted snow away from the bottom edge to allow his bulk to squeak through into the darkness.

He swept his strange purple light over the same scene as before. A computer desk piled with monitors all connected together to monitor what?

Nick followed the cables as they dripped down from the desk and snaked across the floor. He shifted deeper into the room, following the line of cables as they branched across the space. One line scaled the wood wall to his left and ended in a small round surveillance camera mounted near the ceiling, its shiny dark eye aimed straight at the metal cage.

More cables continued to run along the floor in a thick bundle, disappearing into the pile of rubble that blocked the tunnel entrance. Nick shined his light over the pile of rocks climbing higher and higher toward the ceiling. His light froze at the crest of the pile where there was a gap between the wooden braces framing the tunnel and the pile of fallen rocks.

The empty space looked bigger. Before he remembered the space to be about a foot square. Now, it appeared to have grown, tripled it seemed. He played the light into the darkness of the hole and soon realized he was holding his breath.

Keys. He thought. *Keys.*

Nick shuffled across the concrete floor to the cell door and examined the ring of keys in the lock. The ring was oversized and reminded him of the keys they always seemed to use for jail cells in old westerns. There were three keys on the ring and they were all for the cell.

Nick swore under his breath and then turned his attention back to the computer desk. He sat down in the rolling desk chair and pulled open both drawers but found nothing of value.

A few sheets of paper with scrawled notes and designs of what looked like a rough sketch of the cell, a few pens and a half pack of Juicy Fruit. Nick was so tired he felt like he was going to cry. Tears burned at the corners of his eyes as he leaned back, allowing the squeaking wheels of the chair to transport him a foot backwards toward the stone wall.

Defeated he allowed his light to play over the floor and the spilled shotgun shells that littered the ground.

Shotgun shells?

Nick stood and shuffled over to the steel green cabinet with its door swung wide. Inside the gun case there were more boxes of ammunition but no guns.

Nick changed gears and swept his light over the tiny shelves inside the safe. Nothing.

He slammed the narrow door closed and there, hanging from the lock was a collection of keys.

Nick twisted the gun safe key from the lock and examined the rest of them. A couple smaller keys had to be lock boxes, some looked like house keys, but he focused on the only one he needed. A skinny key bearing the blue oval and FORD's clear white signature in the center.

"Thank you Jesus."

Rocks clattered nearby and Nick jumped, nearly dropping the keys and the UV flashlight. The sound exploded in the confined space like a shotgun blast.

Nick spun toward the sound and pinned his light on a rock the size of a Halloween pumpkin that had rolled to a stop ten feet from where he stood. Shaking, his light quivered up over the scree of fallen stones and took aim at the shadow, the hole, at the top of the pile.

Everything stopped. Dust motes swirled through the trembling purple light. Nick strained to listen, desperate to hear nothing at all. To believe that the mountain simply shifted, and the rock, that was balancing precariously to begin with, had finally reached its tipping point and due to physics and nothing more, rolled down the pile to where it lay.

A soft cloud, a ragged handful of breath, drifted through the violet light and disappeared. Nick's stomach twisted and he felt his bladder push against his pelvis.

He dared not move for fear of making a sound.

And then he heard it.

A low grunt. A muffled growl leaked out of the darkness between the stones.

Gripping the ring of keys Nick edged closer to the tunnel entrance, his boots barely scraping across the ground, fixated on a small pale stone.

The rock looked out of place among the rest. Almost white it looked like a chunk of marble tossed in among granite.

Nick shifted his light to see it more clearly and then the white stone sizzled for a split second under scrutiny of the light. It retracted into the dark leaving only a low hiss and the whiff of charred meat in its wake.

A rock exploded out of the shadows, this one no bigger than a football. It whipped past Nick's face so close it ruffled the hair above his right ear and crashed into the computer desk behind him, obliterating one of the monitors. Plastic and glass exploded into the air as the destroyed piece of kit hung off the back of the desk from the wires that connected it to the main terminal.

Another rock, this one larger, the size of a beach ball, soared silently out of the shadows and crashed to the floor a foot from where Nick stood frozen in place.

The roar that thundered out of the buried mine shaft was so loud Nick thought the entire tunnel would collapse along with the bunker. As quick as he could, he back pedalled and fell to the stone floor with a grunt, cracking his right knee on the cement.

He cried out as the flashlight and the keyring were knocked out of his hands. The light spun wildly across the floor revealing the bunker in strobes of purple. He spotted the ring of keys a few feet away and scrambled to collect them first. He dodged another wild stone that smashed into the metal exit door and then scurried toward the flashlight. He scooped it up and the light winked out. He slammed his palm against the side and the violet beam flickered weakly and then died.

Another roar spurred Nick toward the door where a sliver of moonlight spilled inside. Rocks clattered behind him as the roars grew closer. Louder.

He made it to the door and slipped around the gap. The freezing air outside stole his breath and he started to cough so violently he thought his chest would burst. Still, he focused on closing the door behind him. He lowered his shoulder and forced the creaking metal door back toward the wall, but it would not cooperate. He studied the door in the weak light and saw that the barrage of rocks had bent the door itself. The bottom edge of the door now flared out toward the forest.

Again he put his shoulder into the door and pushed, as another rock slammed into the opposite side. Nick squealed as a lightning bolt of pain ran through his shoulder and into his neck and lower back. He bounced away from the door falling backward into the snow as the metal continued to bounce and vibrate in its frame from the attack from within.

Nick scrambled to his feet and kicked the door closed as best he could, not wanting to put his body anywhere near the metal again. When it was as close as he could get it, he forced the top locking bolt closed. Breathing hard he stood back, hands on his knees and stared at the door. The skin was dented and bulging in places, but the top lock was secure. Still the lower edge was angled toward him, but it couldn't be helped.

He had the truck keys now.

They could leave.

They were saved.

Wasting no more time, Nick turned and still clutching the broken flashlight, slipped and stumbled down the path through the trees toward the cabin, and his family.

CHAPTER

THIRTY-FIVE

I
t began as a moan. A low droning sound that rose and fell like the tide.

Ozzy tried to ignore it, poking and prodding at the fire, busying himself with adding more wood to the blaze when required but when she started to scream there was no ignoring her.

The raw desperate shriek stole the breath from his chest and rooted him in place. He felt his full bladder swell, near to bursting. He had been avoiding the hall and the bathroom for the last hour now, hoping his pee would somehow be absorbed by his body through sheer will. He squirmed on the edge of his seat, knowing he couldn't hold it much longer.

Ozzy's eyes flicked to his sister's who had taken to sitting next to their mother on the couch.

"I have to go to the bathroom." He whispered.

"So go."

Ozzy's eyes darted toward the hall and darkness

beyond the range of firelight. He shook his head. His hand drifted to the crotch of his jeans as he squeezed his legs together.

"Ew..." Tara said. "Don't be gross."

"I can't help it."

"Just go." She hissed. "It's fine."

But again Ozzy shook his head, his face a twist of pain.

"Come with me."

Soon a new sound leaked from the darkness and the bedroom beyond. A stream of language as if the woman were speaking to someone in the room, or whispering some ancient prayer. It was too muffled and the words too foreign to decipher.

And then the screaming returned. Bright bursts that jolted Ozzy in his seat.

"Can you get her to stop?" Ozzy asked his sister as he covered his ears. "Please."

Tara ignored him and bent down to examine her mother. Julie had stopped sweating which was good, Tara guessed, and she seemed to be sleeping on and off. Tara checked her mother's bandage and saw that the stumps of her two fingers had stopped bleeding. She thought about changing her sodden bandage when the woman's screams reached a new, ear-splitting pitch.

"*Jesus.*" Tara said.

"Make her stop." Ozzy pleaded. "Please."

Tara climbed to her feet and grabbed the battery powered lantern. She switched it on and the harsh white light chased away the gloom and added new shadows to the walls.

"Come on." She said to Ozzy, holding out her hand. "Let's go."

Ozzy's warm, sweaty hand slipped into her grip and she lead him slowly down the narrow hall.

The volume of the woman's screams dipped for a second and Tara thought it sounded like the woman was praying. The cadence was right, although the words were a mystery. It reminded her of the old Italian women who would whisper the rosary down at St Michael's Church, when their family still went to church. The veiled women all dressed in black would sit near the back, thick knuckles and papery skin expertly slipping the beads between arthritic fingers.

Tara and Ozzy reached the bathroom door and she handed him the lantern. He took it without a word and slipped into the tiny room. He left the door open a few inches, which would have normally grossed Tara out, but in this instance she welcomed the open door, and the sliver of light she was able to stand in.

Nearby, the woman continued to whisper. Strange words drifted out of the dark. Tara could pick out certain words in the maelstrom. Words that sounded like *ratok* and *breeth*, but they meant nothing to her.

Ozzy finished and dutifully flushed the toilet and quickly washed his hands before he nudged open the bathroom door, a weak smile of relief touching his thin lips.

"Better?" She whispered and he nodded.

Ozzy handed his sister the lantern and turned toward the living room, leaving his sister at the bathroom door. He turned when he saw that she wasn't following him. She was heading toward the closed bedroom door.

"What are you doing?" Ozzy asked. "Come on."

But Tara took a step toward the bedroom door and gently laid her hand on the knob.

Ozzy shuffled back toward her, shaking his head.

"*Don't.*"

Tara glared at him in response, her features ghastly and twisted by the harsh fluorescent light of the lantern.

Ozzy stopped in his tracks and waited, unsure how to proceed.

Tara twisted the handle and the door swung open. She held the lantern high and light flooded in.

The smell of urine and something else, something organic wafted through the open doorway forcing Tara to wince.

The woman was where her father had left her, secured to the bed frame, sitting upright. She had kicked away her blanket and the hem of her dirty dress had risen and bunched up just over the dark smudge of her belly button.

The woman's head swung toward the door and Tara saw sweat dripping from the tangles of her hair that were plastered to her face. Her mouth, still stained with her mother's blood hung open and issued a scream of pure agony.

Her slender body slick with sweat twisted and

writhed on the filthy mattress. Her back arched violently. Thick tendons in her neck stood out in stark relief against her flesh. Cords of ropy muscle pulled tight in her slender arms as she struggled against the ropes. Where her father had wrapped them around her wrists Tara saw that her flesh was rubbed raw, the skin red.

Tara felt more than heard, her brother creeping to her side in the dark. She cut her eyes to find his jacked wide. The whites of his pupils clearly visible around the blue of his irises.

"Is she having the baby?" He whispered, his eyes pinned on the woman's stomach as she rocked in place.

Tara angled her light to cast its glare on the woman's belly and saw bulges pushing out from the interior of the woman's body. Indistinct at first, amorphous blobs of something...until she saw the tiny hands. Tiny hands tipped with...*what?*

"*Tara...*" Ozzy whispered and she knew exactly what he was talking about. "*Tara...*"

Tiny hands pressed against the skin of her belly. Delicate pinpricks of pressure scratched against her flesh, as if they were clawing for a way out.

Claws...

Tara felt dizzy. The world was darkening. She couldn't breathe.

The woman screamed again and Tara saw the woman's expression change from pain to terror. She was no longer the spiteful woman teasing and mimicking her from the shadows. She was absolutely frightened. The woman pulled and yanked on her bindings as if she could break free, could outrun what was coming for her.

A mist of crimson painted the yellowing sheets between the woman's legs. Tara and Ozzy yelped in surprise and took a quick step back into the hallway. A torrent of thick red blood followed the initial spray accompanied by the sickening sound of tearing leather.

The woman's head faced the ceiling, the muscles in her throat pulled tight as piano wire and opened her mouth to shriek, but no sound came. A choked, gurgling sound was all Tara could hear before more blood spilled over the woman's lips, running down over her throat to stain the collar of her dress. She spat a mouthful of blood as her eyes searched the dark window. She whimpered, a pathetic, desperate sound as she plead to a god that had abandoned her.

Her body jerked and spasmed as the ripping leather sound continued in fits and spurts. The woman's chin dropped to her chest and remained there, unmoving. Her body still, save for her legs that suddenly kicked out, her heels thrumming on the soiled mattress as tiny hands clawed at the woman's flesh from the inside.

Ozzy grabbed his sister's arm and pulled her, dragging her roughly away from the door. Tara found the door knob without taking her eyes away from the blood soaked bed and slammed the door closed.

THIRTY-SIX

The trees heavy with snow shuddered in the wind and Nick found himself stealing glances over his shoulder back toward the darkness of the bunker.

His feet felt like numb lumps of clay at the ends of his legs and he tripped, falling face first into the drift, his outstretched hands unable to stop his fall. Snow burned his face and spilled down the collar of his coat as he scrambled to his feet. His knee had struck the frozen ground and he was forced to limp once he got upright again.

He still gripped the keys in his gloved hand but he let the useless flashlight lay where it landed.

With no light to guide his way he needed to slow down. The path through the trees was treacherous enough with his torch, but now with only the milky moonlight lighting his way he was all but blind.

The sound of a thin scream twisting through the

darkness spurred him on. He quickened his pace because the scream was coming from the cabin.

MOMENTS LATER NICK emerged from the trees and ran past the half buried pick up truck and climbed up the porch steps. He hit the door hard with his shoulder and then remembered that Tara had locked it behind him. He thundered on the door until her pale face appeared at the tiny window set in the door.

The deadbolt snapped open and Nick pushed his way inside, slamming the door closed behind him. He tore off his scarf and toque and studied the exhausted faces of his children.

Julie had left the couch and was sitting on a chair closer to the fire. Dark circles made her eyes seem small. Her movements were slow and deliberate as if she were moving through water thanks to the Percocets. She clutched her bloody bandage to her chest and slowly found Nick's gaze.

"What's wrong?" He asked the group. "Who was screaming?"

No one responded. No one spoke. His children, his wife, appeared frozen in place. A wax sculpture of his family.

"Julie."

Julie's watery eyes found his and with her chin she gestured down the hall.

"She stopped." Julie whispered.

208

Nick moved to the children and took the dark lantern from Tara. Ozzy was standing behind her, his hand on her wrist, keeping her close.

"Tara?"

"I think she's dead." Tara said quickly.

"What?" Nick asked. "How?"

Tara shook her head, sending tears spilling down her cheeks.

Nick's gaze flicked from Tara to Ozzy who looked to somehow gotten younger. His face looked so small and pale in the flickering firelight.

"Go back to your mom, Oz." Nick told him. "Go on."

Ozzy didn't speak, but he did listen and shuffled away in the dark, taking his sister with him, dragging her behind him. She didn't fight. Together they moved as silent as shadows across the hardwood and knelt down at their mother's feet, close to the fire.

Nick switched on the lantern and moved down the hall. His snowy boots scraped across the floor and left streaks of water in his wake.

He passed the bathroom and pressed his ear to the thin wood of the bedroom door. He heard nothing at first, and then he shifted position and heard...a sound that he hadn't heard in twenty-three years. Not since he spent three weeks at his uncle Jim's farm in upstate Pennsylvania. He had been useless on the farm, and he had been tasked with feeding the pigs. He would carry a dented metal bucket loaded with apple cores and bits of wasted food to the pig pen and dumped it all in the trough. There were three pigs, a sow and two piglets and every day they would rush greedily to the trough, their powerful jaws crushing through every bit of wet slop and bits of bone like so much butter. It was the same sound now. Desperate slurps and...

Jesus, was that chewing?

Nick slipped his hand over the door knob and slowly twisted the handle.

Everything in his mind screamed a single word...

No.

"It's okay." Nick whispered to himself. "It's all right."

He opened the door.

The smell hit him first. A stink coiled out through the narrow gap between the door and the jam. The iron tang of blood and the stink of rot. Nick hesitated on the threshold, the door opened just a few inches, his face pinched in disgust.

The lantern light speared into the room and illuminated the woman's face slumped against her left shoulder. Her black hair was plastered to her skin with sweat and blood and completely covered most of her face and one of her eyes. The visible eye, stared straight into Nick's light, unflinching. Blood had dripped from her slack lips and formed a pool beneath her head.

Nick eased open the door a little wider to find the source of the sounds he heard through the door. He forced the lantern into the gap and angled the beam until he found what he was looking for.

At first he didn't realize what he was looking at. He wondered how animals had gotten into the bedroom, but he wasn't looking at animals. Not really.

The woman's dress was soaked with blood and had been hiked up beneath her breasts in a red twist. Her stomach that had been round and swollen was...*gone*.

No. Not gone. His mind told him. *Not really.*

Instead of her swollen belly criss-crossed with spidery black veins there was something in its place. Her stomach was a ragged wound as if something exploded out of it. As if something had ripped straight through. And something moved in the ruin.

Blood slicked skin and patches of dark hair. Something moving.

Something chewing and slurping. Grunting.

There were two of them.

Nick felt himself falling forward. Unable to stop. Unable to look away.

Christ, they were eating her...

They were children. Toddlers.

He saw them moving, clawing, digging through the shredded husk of their mother, pulling handfuls of flesh and lengths of intestine down deeper into her pelvic cavity where the sounds of their chewing and gorging themselves threatened to bring what little remained in Nick's stomach out onto the floor.

The woman's ribs had been broken with a significant force and her chest was splayed outward. A pile of the woman's steaming entrails had slipped off the end of the bed and were cooling in a wet pile.

The children squeaked and clicked as if speaking to one another.

In a flash they moved as one and slipped out from

between the woman's legs and slammed to the floor in a loose tackle. Sharp black claws tipped their fingers and little toes, digging into the hardwood and gouging out curls of sawdust as they struggled over the last of the entrails, fighting for position.

Nick couldn't help it. The gasp escaped his lips before he could control it and it was enough. The pair of children stopped what they were doing, suddenly aware of Nick's presence, and their faces snapped to the doorway.

Pale and streaked with blood they shared the same deep set eyes like shiny black buttons and large mouths crammed with tiny sharp teeth. Their noses were small and pressed flat to the point of being mostly exposed nostrils. To Nick they looked like pale, wingless bats.

They froze. Their small, wiry bodies held perfectly still, eyes clamped on Nick. Nick wasn't a hunter. He had never killed anything in the wild, but at a glance he knew that he was looking at a pair of predators.

Nick opened his mouth to scream to make some sort of sound but nothing came. What could he say? What would it matter?

Nick stood rooted in place. His hand on the door knob, his breath caught in his throat, his eyes locked on the bloody creatures coiled before him.

The demonic toddlers shrieked in unison, their hungry black eyes still fixed on Nick. Their high pitched scream snapped Nick to attention. Slowly, Nick edged backward as the toddlers eased forward on all fours, eyes up, ready to strike.

Something was happening to their skin.

At first glance it was pink and streaked with gore but there was something else...there was movement beneath their skin. Sinewy worms of muscle squirmed beneath their flesh. While he stared thin muscles formed on biceps and lined their tiny stretching quadriceps.

Were they getting bigger?

Nick watched them stalk slowly across the hardwood on all fours. Liquid rubies of blood dripping from their wet mouths. Their skin was darkening, stretching.

Christ...

They were growing right in front of his eyes.

Shoulders swelled and their backs broadened as they inched toward him across the six feet of floor space.

They were hunting.

How were they hunting? How were they growing so fast?

Nick watched the child closest to him shift its body placing both of its hands on the blood splattered floor. The black tips of its fingernails were the size of small talons now. The monstrous child dug its nails into the wood as it prepared to launch itself.

The twin monsters were coiled like a spring.

Nick had to move. Had to do something.

Still they edged closer until he could smell the gore on them. The whole room smelled like a slaughterhouse.

The child on the left pushed off of the floor and leapt at Nick swiping its clawed hands inches from his face.

Nick stumbled backward and slammed the door closed. The child or whatever the hell it was slammed bodily into the thin wood rattling the door in its frame. It shrieked and screamed and clawed at the opposite side like a rabid dog.

Nick felt the second little monster crash into the door and heard the thin wood veneer split and crack. They were going to break down the door.

"What the fuck?!" Nick screamed as he pulled on the door knob, desperately holding the door closed. "What the actual fuck?!"

CHAPTER

THIRTY-SEVEN

"What is it? What's in there?" Tara asked from the edge of the hall. "What is it?"

Nick strained against the doorknob as the creatures on the opposite side scratched and clawed at the thin barrier between them. Splinters of wood snuck between the gap of the door and the floor.

"Dad?" Tara said.

"I don't know." Nick snapped. "I just need you to find some rope so we can tie this door closed."

"Rope? Where?" Tara said. "Where am I supposed to find rope?"

Something heavy slammed into the door, about chest high and Nick skidded back, losing his footing. He straightened and adjusted his grip on the doorknob.

What the hell?

"In the spare bedroom." Nick yelled. "By the crates, there's some rope. Go now."

Still Tara stood frozen at the end of the hall with

Ozzy nearby. Their eyes flicked to the dark end of the hall past the trembling bedroom door.

"Now!"

Finally, Nick's booming voice in the close confines of the cabin jolted Tara into action and she broke free of Ozzy. She jogged past her father, her gaze barely landing on the door as wood cracked and snapped and splinters and sawdust accumulated around her father's feet.

"Take this." Nick told her and handed her the lantern. She accepted it without a word and continued to the spare bedroom.

Ozzy remained at the edge of the hallway, peering down toward the dark end of the hallway where his father stood in the shadows. His face was a small pale oval in the dark.

Nick felt the knob turn in his sweaty grip.

That's impossible.

But it wasn't. It was happening. Nick squeezed harder, but the knob still turned. Nick held his breath, and focused all his strength, but it didn't matter. The knob turned and then he heard a quiet click.

The door was roughly pulled backward into the bedroom and took Nick with it. Nick propped his boot against the frame and hauled backwards, leaning into the work. The door closed again and the catch clicked into place as the creatures roared in frustration.

The door trembled in the frame as one or both of the monsters worked at the handle with considerable strength from the opposite side, bending the metal lever in his grasp.

He felt himself losing as his sweaty hands slid on the warm metal. He doubled his efforts and leaned further back into the hall, keeping every ounce of his two hundred and thirty-three pounds dangling from the end of that knob.

Inside the furious monsters shrieked and screamed. Their howling chorus reminiscent of their mother and the wailing pleas she belted out before her death.

Is it language?

Nick could swear he could hear words in their cries. Words and phrases bounced back between the two horrific offspring or was it to something else.

Someone else?

Again the monsters threw themselves at the door forcing a crack to appear on Nick's side of the door. He imagined the interior of the door was all but destroyed.

The muscles in Nick's arms and shoulders were burning from the effort. His sore hands had cramped and formed hooked talons around the tiny brass knob.

And then the screaming, wailing cries stopped.

For a moment the sudden silence dropped over them like a shroud. Expanding and filling the space. Nick willed himself not to loosen his grip. He tensed waiting for the next assault. When nothing came he waited still.

"Did they give up?" Ozzy whispered.

Nick shot a glance at his son, who had moved a few steps closer to his position in the quiet.

"Tara, come on with the rope." Nick said. "Please honey."

A moment later Tara returned from the spare

bedroom, a length of orange climbing rope dangling from one hand and the lantern in the other. Her eyes were red and her face was shiny from fresh tears.

"This...is all...I could find." She said, her words coming out halted, catching in her throat as she held out the tangle of rope.

"It's good. It's perfect." He whispered. "Find the end."

Tara set down the lantern and with shaking hands she pulled and sifted through the tangle until she found the end.

Ozzy was nearly on top of them now. His footsteps barely whispers across the floor. His brown eyes pinned to the cracked bedroom door.

"Where did they go?"

And then they heard it.

It was far away, and drifted in and out of their range of hearing but Nick instantly recognized what it was. He had heard it before. He had heard it coming from the bunker.

It was an animal roar that rumbled out of the dark like summer thunder. A deep bass growl he could feel in his chest.

And it was coming closer.

The familiar howl came again. Slightly closer this time. Nick braced himself and quickly adjusted his hands as the creatures behind the door flew into a frenzy, spurred on by the sound of reinforcements. Something was coming. Something like them. Something that answered their cries.

The beaten door creaked and splintered and Nick saw the top hinge was being pulled from the frame, the screws ripping right out of the wood.

It was only a matter of time before the creatures breached the door. The useless shotgun shells burned a hole in his pocket. He needed to get a weapon. A knife. Something. But first he needed to secure this door.

"Ozzy." Nick said suddenly, snapping the boy's head up as if on a string. "Make sure the front door is locked okay. The windows too."

Ozzy nodded silently and then disappeared from the end of the hall.

"Nick?"

Julie appeared at the end of the hall, barely more than a shadow in the waning firelight. Her bloody hand cradled against her chest. Her face the color of milk.

"Nick, what's happening?"

CHAPTER

THIRTY-EIGHT

Before Nick could begin to answer, to even formulate a place to start to explain what had transpired in the last few minutes, the thin plywood that formed the hallway side of the door buckled outward. Nick yelped awkwardly and shuffled his feet back farther from the door. Tara shrieked and scurried further down the hall, the rope abandoned.

"Tara." Nick snapped. "Find the end of the rope."

Crying again, her thin back shuddering in the candle-light, Tara dropped to all fours and yanked the dropped rope toward her, away from the trembling bedroom door.

"Nick what's in there?" Julie asked, taking a step toward him down the hall.

"Please, Julie." He said, his voice strained. "Stay back. Go back to the couch."

At his feet Tara thrust the end of the climbing rope to her father.

"Okay. Good." He told her. "I need you to make a slip knot. Can you do that?"

She nodded and went to work, winding the end of the rope around the longer part and tying it off. Nick watched her progress as he held the door knob as it began to twist again. She completed the knot and held it up for inspection.

"Good."

While holding the doorknob with one hand he took the loop and slipped it around the handle and yanked the knot tight around the metal knob. With it secure he held the slack and waved Tara to move, closer to her mother.

"Okay," he told Tara. "Get back."

Nick wound the rope around his wrist and, while holding the rope tight he played out more and more as he stepped down the hallway, playing the rope out slowly behind him until he was inside the bathroom.

He dropped to his knees and wound the end of the rope around the base of the toilet. As quick as he could he pulled the slack tight as a guitar string and then fashioned a quick knot. The door was anchored by the toilet bowl bolted to the floor.

Claws continued to scratch and carve their way through the weak wood, but the door wouldn't open.

At least not until they broke the handle off. Nick thought.

"Nick, what the hell is that?" Julie asked from the dark, her good hand wrapped around Ozzy's shoulders. Nick tore his eyes away from the door to the master bedroom to find his family huddled behind him. Tara, a few inches taller than Julie standing behind her mother, her pale face hovering over her mother's shoulder.

"Nick."

"I don't know." Nick spat, a little too quickly. He was shaking and tears were burning at the corner of his eyes. "I don't know."

The creatures on the opposite side of the door began pushing on the plywood door and when the wood finally split it sounded like a pistol crack in the silent cabin. The Jacksons jumped and Tara yelped, sparking another crying fit.

Tara hugged her mother fiercely and wept into her shoulder, as if not looking at the door would somehow make the problem go away.

Julie watched with a dazed expression, her expression flat as a pale hand tipped with black razor sharp claws pushed the bottom left corner of the bedroom door away from the frame.

The hand slipped through the gap and probed the rough frame of the door and trim, leaving streaks of crimson blood on the light oak.

"This isn't happening." Nick whispered. "This isn't fucking happening."

Julie watched the hand disappear back into the bedroom and then the door shuddered as something heavy and strong thundered into it from the other side.

"They're gonna break the door down." Ozzy said.

Nick knew it. The door was weak to begin with. It was a miracle it lasted this long.

Nick's heart hammered against his chest as his fingers dug at the chunky ring of keys he had stuffed in his pocket.

We have to go. Now.

"What is that?" Julie whispered, her glazed expression aimed at the crumbling bedroom door.

Nick didn't like the look on her face. Her face was normally expressive and alive. After seventeen years of marriage he could tell what she was thinking from a simple look. The way she squinted her eyes or even tilted her head. But that Julie was gone. The woman that stood before him now was a mystery. A blank slate. Her vacant expression and dull blue eyes like river stones gave him nothing.

He knew she was scared, but it was something else. It looked as though the events of the night had done more to Julie than her wounds would suggest. Everything that had happened so far had hollowed her out. Scooping out everything he knew about her and left him with this shell. He wondered how many Percocets she'd taken.

Nick ripped the keys from his pocket and heard his coat tear in the process. Bits of blue thread and a clump of white stuffing were caught in the ring that held the keys together.

"We're leaving." Nick said, turning to his family. Julie looked right through him.

"I found the keys, Jules."

Julie's eyes flicked from the horror at the end of the hallway to the jumble of keys clenched in her husband's hand and something flickered behind her eyes. Something alive.

It was only a spark, but at this point Nick would take what he could get.

Ozzy ran to grab Julie's coat from the couch and helped her into it. She slid her bloody hand through the sleeve without even a wince and Nick joined the two ends of her zipper together and then zipped her up.

Behind them the bedroom door cracked outward again and the creatures squealed horribly as their claws scrambled across the splintered wood. Julie couldn't stop looking down the hall.

"Don't look, Julie." He told her. "Look at me." Nick held his wife's chin in his hands and gently lead her away to the front door where the kids were already gathered.

Nick pulled Julie's toque down over her head and made sure her ears that had a tendency to poke out from her blonde hair were tucked under the hat.

"Good." Nick whispered, as he stroked his wife's cheek. "It's all right."

Nick turned to the front door where Tara and Ozzy stood at the window staring out into the blizzard. Their posture was all wrong. They were not excited and ripping open the door.

Something had changed.

"Let's go." Nick said, "Open the door."

The kids didn't respond, even as the screaming grew louder from the bedroom and wood splintered and cracked like thunder behind them.

"Tara open the fucking door."

Ozzy turned to his father and raised a small right hand and pointed out at something through the window. Something in the darkness.

Nick stepped closer, his breath fogging up the window. Outside behind the porch was the mound of the Professor's truck half buried in snow. The wind was still strong and at its peak he couldn't see much past the front fender that peeked out from the storm.

The wind changed and a howl erupted from outside. An animal roar that stole the breath from his lungs and fired his heart into a higher gear.

Something was out there.

It stood just beyond the warm glow of the cabin. A hulking figure with broad shoulders and long powerful arms that dangled past its waist. The creature roared again, its hot breath smoking in the weak light.

"Get away from the door." Nick said, his mouth as dry as sand.

The door to the master bedroom shuddered in the frame as the monsters on the opposite side forced their arms through the breaks, desperate to get through.

"What is happening, Dad? What is that?" Tara asked, staring through the frosted window.

Nick had no answers. He just shook his head. The keys to the truck, worthless now clenched in his fist.

Julie turned to her husband, her expression vacant, her eyes dead.

"It's coming for its children." She said.

CHAPTER

THIRTY-NINE

N
ick edged closer to the window, his hot breath fogging up the glass, clouding his view of the outside, but not enough.

The figure stood perfectly still and if it were any other night, in any other place, the thing might pass for a gnarled tree. But not tonight. Slowly, it tilted its head toward the sound of the monstrous children in the back bedroom. Their cries spurred the thing on, toward the cabin.

It moved so fast, so incredibly fast that Nick lost sight of it in the shadows.

Movement to his left, beyond the truck bed, snared Nick's attention.

Jesus Christ...

There's more.

Two more at least, smaller than the first, but still as big as a man, and moving closer, dipping cat-quick in and out of the shadows.

"Holy shit." Nick muttered. "Oh God."

"Who are they?" Ozzy asked. "What do they want?"

Outside the three figures slipped silently between the truck and the cabin, cutting off their escape.

Nick had no answer for his son.

Ozzy moved into position next to his father, peering into the dark. Nick grabbed him roughly by the shoulder and pulled him away from the window.

"Get away from the windows."

"They're coming inside." Julie moaned. "They're coming in here."

Julie gathered her children to her, moving slowly back toward the warmth and the light of the dying fire. She spied a butcher's block full of knives on the counter and gripped a long, thin-bladed filleting knife.

Shotgun shells.

The words flashed as red neon in Nick's mind.

Shotgun shells.

Nick's hand moved to his pocket and felt the familiar shape. He needed a weapon. Now.

Nick bolted down the hallway with the lantern, past the ruined door, and past the crooked pale fingers reaching through. Pale fingers splashed with blood. Fingers and hands that could not possibly belong to the two things that were just spawned in that room. Fingers tipped with black claws.

The fury and the chittering language that exploded from the room buzzed in his head, and pushed at his temples, biting into his brain.

He kept moving and slipped into the spare bedroom.

227

He lowered the lantern to keep the glare off of the window and through the glass on the western wall he caught a glimpse of movement outside.

Nick couldn't help but stare at the dark figure cloaked in shadow running on all fours. Kicking up snow in its wake, galloping through the drifts and disappearing into the darkness.

Nausea rolled in his stomach.

This can't be happening.

He had to focus. He moved to the closet and opened the door to the green metal gun safe and ripped open the door.

Two guns remained. An older pump action shotgun, matte black and a newer black handgun.

Nick selects the shotgun. It's been forever since he loaded or even held a shotgun, but the practiced movements return quickly. He found a box of the shells on the cabinet shelf and started feeding the red, copper capped tubes one at a time into the breech. When the capacity was met, he stuffed the extra shells into the pockets of his coat.

Next he lifted the handgun from its peg and found the word GLOCK stamped along the side. A weapon he'd only heard about in movies and TV shows.

His hands were shaking but after a few failed attempts, he found the magazine release and ejected the ammo clip. Shiny brass bullets winked out of the darkness and Nick saw that the ammo clip was fully loaded. He slammed the clip back into the grip and racked the slide before he stuffed the gun into the pocket of his parka.

Something like confidence swelled inside him. Building. He lifted the shotgun and the deadly weight reassured him. He could feel the odds of their survival begin to slowly tip in their favor. He can do this. They could leave now.

They are fucking out of here.

CHAPTER

FORTY

Nick swept into the hallway, the shotgun clutched in a two handed grip, the barrel swinging toward the shattered bedroom door. Pale arms, impossibly long...

They're only children...

...tipped with grasping hands the color of bone streaked with blood that clawed at the air, searching for something. Anything.

Flesh.

The lantern's glow swept over the door spearing harsh light through the cracks illuminating the crouching creatures pressed against the crumbling wood. Two sets of dark wet eyes ringed in red, the color of their mother's, glared at him with murderous intent. Their chittering language punctuated with spit and sour drool that leaked from their mouths corrupted the silence of the cabin.

The door knob lay at an angle, twisted and bent. The

climbing rope anchoring the knob to the toilet hung limp allowing the door to open a few inches. The creatures' fury rose, the door shook shedding bits of wood into the hall.

It wouldn't be long now.

At the front door Tara and Ozzy's eyes flicked to the shotgun in Nick's hands but they said nothing. Julie barely glanced at the weapon, her mind spinning on something else. Something far away.

Any thought of giving Julie the handgun weighing down his parka pocket was abandoned. He imagined handing her the pistol and watching it slip from her fingers, clattering to the ground, useless.

They needed to focus.

They needed to leave. Now.

"We're leaving." Nick said. "Right now."

"How?" Tara wanted to know. "With those things out there?"

Nick transferred the keys to the truck into his right coat pocket and then turned to his wife.

"You still have your little flashlight?"

Julie blinked and stared at him.

"Julie." Nick said again, louder this time. *"Your flashlight?"*

Julie's left hand moved agonizingly slow, from cradling her wounded right, to her pocket, as if she were underwater. She pulled the tiny black flashlight from her pocket and handed it to Nick.

"Where did you get a shotgun?" She asked dreamily, studying the weapon.

Nick took the flashlight and handed it to Tara. Tara accepted it with both hands and still looked confused.

"Ozzy." Nick said, "You open the door when I tell you. Tara, you are the light. We're gonna move to the truck all together and we're all gonna get in. Julie, Ozzy and Tara on this side of the truck and I'm gonna get in to drive."

"What if they're out there?" Ozzy said, squeezing closer to his mother.

"We have to go." Was all Nick said. "Now."

"What if the truck won't start." Tara asked.

"It'll start." Nick told her without making eye contact, without showing doubt.

"But if it doesn't? We'll be trapped in a truck instead of in here." Tara asked.

"Listen to me. We have to leave. We can't stay here." He said to all three of them.

"We can barricade ourselves in." Ozzy pleaded. "We can stay in here where it's warm until it gets light out."

But Nick was already shaking his head.

"They're gonna come inside." He said, cutting off his son. "They're gonna get in and then we won't have an option."

A chorus of shrieks and more of the chittering language exploded from the bedroom. High pitched squeals and clicks followed by a deeper reply, desperate, rage fuelled scream. This new sound was not the children.

The bedroom door thundered in its frame as hundreds of pounds struck it from the opposite side. The knob bent and snapped free from the cheap plywood door as the door swung inward, and darkness flooded into the light.

Nick swung the barrel toward the hall as shadows spilled into the gloom. Nick didn't wait. He fired. The deafening blast exploded in the small space illuminating the hallway and the thin, bone-white thing that emerged from the doorway. For a moment the creature's gore streaked face shone in the flash, hissing and screeching, and then it was thrown backward, deeper into the darkness.

"Open the door, Ozzy." Nick said. "Let's go!"

But Ozzy buried his face into his mother's chest, pushing himself deeper into her body, looking for a place to hide. To escape, shaking his head.

Nonononononononono

The cabin filled and expanded with a chorus of screams and shrieks. Nick racked another shell into the breech, the expended casing spinning away toward the couch and the dying fire beyond.

"Now, Ozzy goddamn it!" Nick thundered, raising the shotgun and aimed back toward the bedroom, waiting for something to emerge from the dark. *"Open the door!"*

Finally, Tara stepped past her paralyzed brother and grabbed the door knob. Her shaking fingers were all but useless, but she managed to grab the deadbolt, unlock the door and twist the knob.

"Ready?" Nick said.

No one was. A cloud of fear surrounded them like a poisonous gas.

Nick nodded, mostly to himself. Getting ready. Psyching himself up.

Gripping the shotgun with both hands, still aimed down the darkened hallway.

"Okay, open it, Tara."

Julie gripped Ozzy close to her chest, her eyes finally showing some glimmer of life as they flicked from the darkened hallway to the front door.

Nick covered the hallway with the shotgun trembling in his grip. He cheated a glance over his shoulder toward the front door and his daughter's face shiny with tears. Her thin hands wrapped around the door knob.

Nick nodded to Tara and she opened the door. Shards of ice and snow whipped into the cabin through the open portal.

Tara was the first to see it.

Her scream yanked Nick's head around on his neck. His body followed, but slower. He wrenched the barrel of the shotgun toward the shape charging out of the darkness.

Standing twenty feet away was what looked like a man, but much taller. A gnarled oak that has pulled its roots from the ground and has learned to run. Its powerful body was covered in something dark and textured. Mud and dried blood mixed with bits of tree bark.

It charged into the lantern light that streamed from the open cabin door, toward the warmth of the cabin and the huddle of terrified people.

It took forever for Nick to wheel around, dragging the

shotgun through the frigid air as if he were moving through tree sap. The figure had no such trouble. The black lips of the creature's impossibly wide mouth opened baring distinct rows of jagged teeth dripping with strings of flesh and strands of ropy saliva.

Ten feet away Nick could smell it now. Rotten meat and unwashed flesh, it moved in a cloud of its own stink and Nick was reminded of his uncle's hog farm. The grunting mass of muscle and bone, struggling for scraps. Sharp teeth gnashing and tearing.

Nick raised the shotgun and his finger yanked the trigger. The gunshot exploded but the shot was wide, hitting the passenger window of the truck, the glass exploding in a shower of falling stars.

Unfazed the creature charged, powerful arms and legs moving with hateful machine precision. It propelled itself at Nick's family like a cruise missile.

The figure roared, its arms open wide, razor tipped hands reaching, as it closed the gap between the truck and the front door. It bounded up the porch steps in one massive leap and Nick pulled the trigger again.

This time he was too close to miss.

The blast ripped through the creature's left shoulder spinning the beast off its trajectory. Crimson blood sprayed into the winter wind as the monster spun away, off of the porch steps and into the darkness below.

Nick loaded another shell and screamed, "Back! Back! Get back inside!"

In the shadows the creature howled and scrambled to its feet, peering cautiously over the edge of the porch.

Hesitant now, Nick could just see the filthy dome of its head, and the flicker of its eyes, but it was enough. Nick let loose another shotgun blast, obliterating the wooden railing and a fist sized chunk of the deck.

The creature bolted, retreating into the darkness, scurrying through the snow to the rear of the truck and disappearing.

"Fuck!"

More shadows slunk through the darkness on his right. Drawn by the sound, their high keening shrieks rising over the wind.

"Get back!" Nick screamed, pushing the herd of his family backward.

Movement all around now. Shadows peeled away from the darkness and were converging on the front porch.

"Go! Now!"

Nick pulled the trigger and the shotgun spat fire, a lightning strike in the night. A smaller thinner creature howled and collapsed to the right of the truck's fender, its knee a ragged mess of stringy red muscle and torn flesh. It writhed in the snow turning red around it, struggling to get to its feet, to get at Nick.

Nick ripped his eyes away from the horde clamouring into the light and slammed the cabin door closed before what felt like a train hit the opposite side. The thunderous blow bounced Nick's two hundred and thirty-three pounds a foot backward.

Julie and Nick and Tara and Ozzy rushed back toward the door, their legs extended, knees bent, and with their shoulders lowered, they smashed the creature's fingers in the gap between the door and the frame. The monster squealed but the Jacksons didn't relent.

Nick edged closer to the door and found a second effort, slamming the door closed on the beast's trapped fingers. Bones cracked and blood squirted from the ruined digits until with a final push the door closed. The catch clicked into place and Nick snapped home the deadbolt.

Three bloody fingers dropped to the hardwood with a wet splat, rolling in lazy circles until they came to rest in a neat little row.

With his back to the door Nick swept the barrel of the shotgun over the cabin, probing the darkness beyond the cone of light thrown from the lantern.

The dying firelight flickered in the hearth casting its own shadows across the floor.

Nick concentrated on listening, listening for their attack. Waiting for them to pounce, to strike, but the only sound beyond the howling wind outside was the low crackle and snap of the fireplace and the ragged, panicked breathing of his family huddled in a nervous ball against the kitchen cupboards.

CHAPTER

FORTY-ONE

I n the kitchen Nick crouched down next to his family, painfully gripping the shotgun, his knuckles white and aching. Julie had one arm wrapped protectively around Ozzy who couldn't stop crying, his face buried into her shoulder. She rubbed the back of his neck with her left hand as his back shuddered, silent sobs causing his whole body to quake and shiver.

Tara squatted on her haunches nearby, her back against the kitchen cabinets. The thin beam of her flashlight probing the semi-dark of the cabin. First toward the front door.

The door was still and the creatures beyond, silent, for the time being, and then to the large dark window overlooking the driveway and the forest beyond. The black glass revealed nothing of the outside. It reflected the flickering light of the fire and the distant dots of candles left burning around the living area: the professor's desk, the kitchen island, the low end table to the right of the couch.

The beam of her pale light trembled as it crept down the hallway, catching motes of dust and larger bits of ash. It slid toward the ravaged bedroom door that hung from one ruined hinge and across the splinters and chunks of wood and shiny pinpricks of bent nails that littered the floor.

Nick rose slowly from his crouch, his rusting joints creaking and popping with the effort. He was not made to crouch and his knees sizzled with pain that burned up and down his legs.

"Nick..."

Julie's whisper was a hiss in the gloom.

"Stay down."

But Nick ignored her. He had to. He'd heard something. A faint clicking noise. Somewhere close.

Something was moving in the wreckage of the hall. Slowly, his eyes flicked from the hall to the front door and to the large rectangular window to his left, just begging to be smashed. In fact he was surprised it hadn't been destroyed already. He checked the dark glass for movement. For shadows darting behind its glossy black surface, but saw nothing. He could feel his heartbeat in his ears and he quickly wondered if his heart would give out before the monsters killed him.

"Dad..." Tara said, her voice tight with concern.

Nick followed the white light of her beam and saw the pieces of the door that lie in the hallway, including the doorknob, still tied to the orange climbing rope.

Nick stared at the pool of light not understanding what he was looking at.

What is that?

Curls of wood had formed a small pile on the floor. Wooden shavings.

Tara shifted her light and found more of the same. Chunks of wood, splinters and sawdust like a trail of breadcrumbs dotted the floor, edging deeper into the living room.

A small chunk of wood, no bigger than a toothpick, dropped through the dark, and through the shaft of her light and hit the hardwood floor with soft *click*.

Tara angled her light up higher, following the trajectory of the splinter to the wood beam ceiling where a bald creature with pale skin and barely formed features hung upside down from the rafters.

If this is the child, it has grown since Nick last saw it. *Exponentially*. The creature looked to be at least four feet tall now. Long and thin with ropy muscles pulled tight over a skeleton that was growing and creaking in real time. Tendons like piano wires pulled tight around the monster's throat. Its entire translucent skin was crisscrossed with a spidery network of black veins and blood vessels.

The light speared the monster straight in its black eyes and it shrieked in pain, curling back its black lips and gnashing its rows of needle like teeth. Tara held the thing in her beam, her arm locked out straight, as if she could somehow trap it there.

With every shift of the creature's black fingernails

and that of its feet, it gouged out more little curls of wood, showering the floor below.

"Kill it!" Julie screamed from the floor. "Kill it, Nick!"

Nick raised his shotgun and took aim at the squealing monstrosity hanging from the ceiling.

The front door shuddered in the frame and Nick flinched, pulling his shot wide. Wood exploded inches from the shrieking beast's face. It dropped heavily to the floor and raced out of sight, heading toward the corner of the room and the protection of the professor's desk.

Nick fired again and the blast tore a fist sized chunk out of the professor's oak desk and obliterated the fat yellow candle that sat there. A tongue of flame and a pint glass of hot wax splashed onto the thick red drapes instantly lighting them ablaze.

The pounding on the door stopped and something big passed by the window, nothing but a darker shadow against the blackness.

Nick swivelled the shotgun barrel toward the hallway where a second squealing creature charged headlong on all fours. Its devilish head was raised and its black eyes were fixed on Nick. Nick fired without aiming and the creature's left arm disappeared below the elbow in a red mist. The creature squealed in pain and collapsed in a writhing heap. Its chittering language screaming and shrieking, as its head swivelled back toward the hallway and the ruined door of the bedroom.

Nick didn't have to aim. He was too close to miss. He fired another round into the back of the beast's bald head whipping back and forth against the floor. In a brilliant flash of light the creature shuddered once and then went still, brackish blood pooling around the ruin of its head.

"Get up!" Nick yelled. "Let's go! Up!"

Julie was the first to her feet, dragging Ozzy behind her. Tara swept her flashlight over the professor's desk and pinned the top of the creature's bald pate and a single hateful eye.

"Dad!"

Nick aimed at the dot of light and fired. Chunks of wood streamed into the air as smoke and the smell of spent gunpowder filled the room. He had no idea if he hit the thing, but it wasn't the point. With the door left unguarded, it was time to leave.

Nick stumbled backward, digging another shell out of his coat pocket and stuffing it into the breech. He did all this without taking his eyes off of the hallway and somehow, the professor's shattered desk in the corner of the room. The shell slid home, Nick cocked the action and fired, punching a fist-sized hole in the drywall.

THE JACKSONS HEARD the sound of shattering glass coming from the master bedroom before a guttural roar erupted from the darkness, freezing everyone in their place.

Nick waved Tara to the door as he unlocked the deadbolt. He spun, keeping his back to the wall beside the door, and his shotgun trained on the living room behind him, as Tara gripped the door handle.

He found her eyes in the dim light and nodded

quickly. She opened the door and Nick led with the shotgun. Snow and wind and needles of ice stung his face but
there was no one waiting for them. No one lurking at the
end of the porch steps.

He leaped down the three steps and jogged through
the snow.

"Get in!" He cried. "Get in!"

The doors on the passenger side of the truck were
unlocked and Nick heard the doors open, the creaking of
the ancient hinges and then the doors slam closed
behind them, as he raced around to the driver's side,
shotgun up and ready.

Shadows flicked through the swirling snow, but
nothing attacked. Nothing approached.

Nick wrenched open the driver's side door and
dropped behind the wheel. He handed the shotgun to
Julie who grabbed the stock and awkwardly angled it
into the footwell.

Nick's gloved hands were too clumsy to find the truck
keys and he needed to strip them off before he could
locate them. He bit the end of the sodden glove and
ripped his hand free. His fingers closed over the chilly
metal of the keys as Ozzy screamed.

"They're coming!"

FORTY-TWO

N ick's eyes flicked to the cabin as a torrent of darkness flooded through the front door. Julie screamed and twisted and launched herself across her seat and toward Nick, smashing into him and nearly causing him to drop the keys.

Behind him Ozzy and Tara were huddled together and screaming for Nick to start the *goddamn* truck.

The biggest creature thundered down the porch steps and ran at the truck like it was going to tackle it. It lowered its shoulder and drove a ham-sized fist into the rear passenger window. The truck shuddered with the blow and the glass splintered, but didn't break.

"Go! Go! Go!" Julie screamed, her back pressed tight against Nick, her boots wedged flat against her own door.

Nick stabbed the key into the ignition as the monster punched the window again. This time the cracks spider-webbed outward, but still the window held.

244

Nick cranked the ignition and the engine whined as the headlights flickered to life, and then, with a wheeze, the engine chugged and died. More monsters glided through the shadows illuminated by the yellow glow of the truck's headlights, and then disappeared from view.

"NO!" Nick screamed. "No!"

Again he cranked the key, twisting it hard enough to break the end off in the ignition, and pumped the gas, praying to any god who was listening for this one thing. This one break.

The creature roared outside Tara's window fogging the splintered glass and it struck the window again. A blizzard of safety glass blew into the backseat pelting the cowering children as the engine caught and flared to life.

The headlights blazed in the dark and the three smaller creatures scuttled for the safety of the shadows between the trees.

A huge pale hand tipped with long black claws reached in through the shattered window and grabbed at Tara's leg. She screamed and squirmed on her seat, desperate to get far enough away, to be out of the reach of the monster. But its hand found her ankle and clamped around it like a vise, its nails digging through her jeans and into the soft flesh of her calf.

Tara screamed as she was yanked toward the broken window. Ozzy gripped his sister under her arms but he was not strong enough to hold her back. The monster yanked her again and pulled the two of them toward the passenger window.

"Mom!" Ozzy screamed. "Mom!"

Julie spun in her seat and grabbed Tara's coat sleeve with her undamaged hand, screaming with the effort.

Nick grabbed the gear shift and dropped it into reverse. He pressed the gas and the tires spun on a layer of snow and ice.

"Come on!" He screamed. Over his shoulder Tara and Ozzy were being dragged toward the open window. Tara screamed as blood soaked the calf of her jeans where the monster's nails tore through skin and scratched across the bones of her shin. Another grunt and shriek from the hideous thing that had latched onto his daughter and her leg, from the knee down, was now outside of the car.

The tires on the truck spun and spun, smoking in the snow and Nick could smell the stench of rubber burning. Julie lost her grip on her daughter and moved to her door, pushing through and dragging the shotgun behind her.

"Julie no!" Nick screamed, but it was too late. Julie was out through the passenger door, raising the shotgun. Nick dropped the truck into park and dug the pistol out of his coat pocket and reached for his own door handle.

Tara was wailing, her one leg was pulled straight through the empty space where the window had been, bleeding into the snow covered ground. The other leg she had propped against the door frame, her boot firmly planted on the inside of the truck cabin as Ozzy pulled her from behind.

"Pull!" Tara screamed and she heard her brother grunt and wail as he leaned backward, desperate to drag her with him.

Julie barely got her boots on the ground when she saw what had grabbed her daughter. For a moment everything stopped. She couldn't breathe or move as her mind struggled to ratify what she was seeing with what she knew to be true.

Tara shrieked again as her jeans ripped. Wounds ran in ragged lines down her smooth, pale calf. Julie raised the shotgun aiming the barrel at the wide chest of the monstrosity. With no index finger she struggled to hold the rifle with her left and squeezed the trigger. There was a click, and nothing else.

Nick ran around the rear of the truck, gun out, looking for a shot in the dark.

Julie's head snapped up as she heard a sharp dry crack. The wail Tara made was inhuman and filled Julie's stomach with ice.

Julie watched in horror as her daughter's body was roughly yanked through the open window as easily as a bag of laundry. The creature allowed Tara to drop into the snow, her complexion matching the winter white. The thigh of her free leg bent at an unnatural angle. Her femur broken and poking through a ragged gash in her blood soaked jeans. Glistening splinters of bone catching sparks of moonlight.

"No!No!No!No!"

Nick screamed, running and slipping in the snow as he turned the corner around the end of the truck, the shaking pistol gripped in one hand looking for a clean shot.

The dark, shifting creature paid Nick no mind as he

hauled Tara's limp body over his shoulder. Her body flapped across the monster's back, her pale face glowing in the weak light. Her mouth opening and closing, searching for breath.

Nick slipped and fell to the ground. Snow sprayed across his face and burned his skin, but he scrambled to his knees, pistol up as Tara finally found the wind to scream, *"Daddy!"*

The creature took off running, loping through the twin headlights and disappearing into the trees.

"Daddy!"

"Tara! TARA!"

Nick struggled to his feet and squinted into the shadows. He knew where the creature went. He can see the monster's oversized footprints punching a path through the snow between the lines of pines.

It was taking her to the bunker. Not just the bunker, Nick knew, the tunnel, and deeper into the mountain.

"DADDY!" Tara's voice knifes through the darkness and spurred Nick into motion.

Julie too has started to move, albeit in a halting, half dazed way, toward the twisting forest. She dragged the shotgun behind her with her good hand, gouging a thin line in the snow.

"Julie!" Nick said. "Wait."

But she didn't. She moved in a steady pace, one foot in front of the other.

"Dad." Ozzy said, as he trembled in the backseat. "I couldn't hold her."

Nick shook his head and wrapped his son up in his arms.

"It's okay." He whispered into his son's hair. "It's okay. Climb in the front and stay low. Don't come out, okay?"

"Where are you going?" He asked.

"I gotta get your sister."

Ozzy's face betrayed something he wished he could say out loud without the crushing guilt it would bring. Nick was thinking the same thing.

"She's coming back." Nick said quickly. "We're all leaving."

Nick squeezed Ozzy one last time and closed the rear passenger door.

"If something comes back...hit the horn, okay?"

Ozzy nodded as he climbed between the front seats of the truck and melted into the shadows of the front passenger footwell, curling into a ball, wrapping his arms around his knees, making himself as small as possible.

"Tara!" Julie screamed. "Tara!"

"Daddy!"

Tara's shriek was bright with pain.

Julie lunged toward the sound now, locking on its location, but Nick had caught up with her and grabbed her shoulder, pulling her back.

"Stay with the truck, Julie. Stay with Ozzy."

Julie stared at him as if he's a stranger, speaking in a language she couldn't understand.

"Julie." Nick tried again. "Stay with Ozzy. I'll get

Tara."

"They took her."

"I know." Nick told her. "I'll find her."

"I can hear her, Nick. I can hear her."

"We're gonna find her." Nick said.

"I'm not leaving without Tara."

"Just let me do this."

"I can help." Julie told him.

"I don't need your help. I need you to stay with Ozzy."

"Daddy!"

Julie lurched toward the sound of her daughter, and took off running, dropping the shotgun in the snow.

"Wait!" He snapped and handed his wife the pistol. "Take this."

Julie's eyes flicked from the pistol in her left hand to her husband, and then finally toward the path through the trees.

A guttural scream twisted out of the dark as the wind flared, shaking the tops of the trees, pulling groans and creaks out of the tortured wood.

Julie was gone. Running as fast as her legs would take her. Soon her shuffling form was quickly eaten by the darkness as she broke through the tree line and headed deeper into the forest.

Nick scooped up the shotgun where Julie had dropped it, and racked a fresh shell into the breech. His legs moved easily beneath him as he picked up speed, but he felt like he was falling more than running, falling into an abyss as he chased his wife into the dark.

CHAPTER

FORTY-THREE

Beneath the canopy of trees the darkness was absolute. Nick slowed to a crawl and then stopped completely when he could hear the ragged breathing of his wife standing next to him. The warm clouds of her breath swirled around his face and he could hear his heart hammering in his ears. He squinted into the blackness, but there was nothing.

He raised the barrel of his shotgun, waiting. Desperate for a direction but nothing came.

"Julie."

And then she was gone, moving blind through the darkness. Nick hurried after her as she pushed through low hanging branches weighted with snow.

Julie screamed, beyond fear and caution and reason now.

"TARA! Tara! Honey where are you?"

Nick and Julie emerged blinking, stunned by the sudden brightness, into a patch of watery moonlight.

The wind moaned through the boughs and needled their faces with tiny daggers of ice. Thirty feet away to their right the green metal door of the bunker hung ajar on its lone hinge, bent and gently swaying in the frigid wind. Directly in front of the door, a smear of crimson stained the snow.

The sound of a car horn whipped their heads toward the way they had come.

Ozzy.

Nick grabbed Julie before she took another step. Their eyes locked, the impossible choice left unsaid.

"Julie...we need to get back...Ozzy..."

"I'm not leaving...TARA!"

Julie ripped her arm out of Nick's grasp and stomped toward the bunker door and the bloody smear in the snow.

The horn blared again and Nick snapped a glance back toward the truck, completely torn. But Julie was running now toward the door. Toward something small lying on the forest floor.

"Tara! Tara!"

Nick ran to catch up, grabbing for Julie, desperate to catch her before she saw, before she recognized what the small something was.

"DADDY!" Tara's bright scream was so close, so real, so scared.

Julie crumbled to her knees, her forward momentum carrying her body, forcing her to skid through the bloody snow. Her hands shook as she reached out, and touched the bloody tangles of her daughter's hair.

Nick's knees gave out and he dropped next to his wife, his shotgun forgotten, a scream trapped in his chest.

He was staring at his daughter's severed head in the snow.

"DADDY!" Tara's voice screamed again in the dark, closer still. "Daddy!"

It's a trap.

Julie's desperate grating wail hit Nick like a blow to the chest. Her trembling fingers swept the strands of hair away from her daughter's cheek. Away from her green eyes fixed on nothing. Her mouth frozen in a scream.

They're coming.

Nick grabbed Julie's coat, yanking her away, pulling her to her feet. Julie fought him, ripping away from his grip, and slamming her body down into the ground.

"No. Julie. We have to go."

"We can't leave her here."

Nick scanned the trees and he swore he could hear the thunder of running footsteps.

"We have to. Come on. Get up!"

Julie ignored him, her eyes fixed on her daughter's, her fingers combing Tara's blood soaked hair.

"Julie!"

Tara's disembodied voice screams again, *"Daddy!"*

"Julie. Come on!"

Nick grabbed Julie again and using all his strength, yanked her to her feet and pulled her back toward the truck.

Ragged grunts and the alien sound of the creatures chittering language swelled in the dark, getting closer.

Nick dragged Julie along, constantly scanning the forest all around them. Something big and dark was pacing them on their left, just beyond the trees.

"Come on! RUN!"

Julie found her feet and her knees pumped up and down as Nick's worried gaze drifted to the left and spotted a dark shadow slip between the trees.

Julie raised her gun and fired two wild rounds into the shadows. The kickback caused her to stumble and she fell, the gun spinning away into the snow.

"Julie! No!"

Nick scrambled to a stop and doubled back as Julie was getting to all fours.

The horn noise was constant now, blaring its droning single note in the dark.

Tears streamed down Julie's face, her body wracked with sobs as she swept her bare hands through the snow in search of the pistol.

"Julie please, honey." Nick begged her, yanking her to her feet. "Please, come on. Keep moving."

Suddenly the horn stopped. Silence flooded in, smothering them.

Oh God.

"Just stay with me, okay." Nick said. "Stay with me."

Julie's eyes were glazed and lost. Her mouth hung slack. Nick squeezed her hand and pulled her toward the truck, one foot at a time, faster and faster.

"Stay with me, honey."

Julie didn't respond.

Nick saw only a blur of grey flesh. Heard a low growl of something charging out of the dark.

Naked and pale with long black hair, the figure exploded out of the shadows with frightening, animal speed.

The figure leapt and tackled Julie straight back into the snow before Nick could even turn.

The creature dropped its crushing weight on top of Julie, squeezing the meagre air from her lungs. Ribs broke like kindling as Julie coughed up lungfuls of blood.

The creature opened its mouth filled with too many jagged teeth and Tara's screams punctured the silence.

"DADDY! DADDY! DADDY!"

Nick swivelled toward the creature as Julie screamed, writhing beneath its massive body.

"Julie!"

Nick aimed at the monster's rippling back and fired. The creature howled as blood erupted from its left shoulder. Nick pumped another round into the barrel and rushed closer.

"Julie!"

The monster snapped its blood soaked face toward Nick, roared and leapt away, disappearing into the forest dark before Nick could line up another shot.

Nick crumbled to Julie's side watching the arterial blood jet from her ravaged face, throat and upper chest. Julie's lower jaw had been ripped away leaving her tongue exposed, flopping uselessly against her chest.

Nick shook uncontrollably now, slipping into shock.

This was all too much. He couldn't take anymore. Julie shuddered, her heels drumming on the frozen ground as the streams of blood slowed to a trickle as she quickly bled out.

This can't be happening.

This isn't happening...

Please...

Julie's eyes dilated into black saucers as her last breath formed a fragile cloud in the moonlit dark and drifted away.

The world went quiet. All sound was replaced by Nick's own screaming and the frenetic drum beat of his heart in his ears.

And then another sound exploded out of the dark.

A horn.

Ozzy.

Nick scrambled to his feet, the soles of his boots slipping in his wife's blood. Scratching and clawing through the bloody snow he righted himself, squeezed the shotgun in his hands and ran like a man possessed toward the truck, and his son, and the sound of the horn.

FORTY-FOUR

Orange light swelled in the darkness detailing the swaying pine trees, lining them with fire. Nick stomped through the snow toward the glow, his legs pumping up and down like pistons. He wasn't worried about the noise he was making or the sound that was leaking from his throat. It wasn't a word, or phrase, but a low moan, a droning battle cry as he lowered his head and punched through the screen of branches.

Flags of fire waved from every window in the cabin and toxic clouds of black smoke billowed from the open door, and had begun to twist up through the chimney and the weaker spots in the roof.

The truck horn sounded again and in the weak light of the flickering flames, Nick could see the small, pale face of his son sitting behind the wheel.

One creature stood facing the truck. Its head bent in

consideration, as if listening to the bleat of the horn and trying to decipher some hidden meaning.

Lit by the blaze behind it, for the first time, Nick can see the creature clearly. Long and lean, its pale, gnarled body is clean of any camouflage worn by the larger, older creatures.

This one was clearly the child.

It stood in front of the truck, between the twin beams of the headlights, staring into the windshield at his son.

Nick raised the shotgun and scanned the dark snow fields beyond the reach of the firelight. Shadows tore away from the darkness on either side, racing silently, converging.

He aimed with one eye closed down the barrel and didn't have a shot. If he missed he could hit Ozzy.

Damn.

With leaden legs and frozen feet, Nick took off running toward the driver's side of the truck and began to scream.

"Hey! Hey! Asshole!"

The creature's head snapped toward the sound. Its face was almost entirely mouth. Its thin black lips curled back revealing rows of ragged teeth. The massive jaws snapped with an audible *clack-clack* and then it was moving, dropping to all fours and charging.

Nick skidded to a stop and took aim.

More creatures were screaming now, adding their voice to the chorus. Nick saw movement out of the corner of his eye but didn't dare turn his head.

He fired.

The shotgun blast thundered over the din of the approaching monsters, but the shot went wild and the pale creature didn't flinch.

Didn't stop.

Arms and legs moving with machine precision it clawed easily through the snow with its head up and fierce red eyes locked on Nick, its jaws clacking loudly, its sharpened black tongue snapping out between its teeth like a striking cobra.

Nick racked another shell into the breech and fired. The creature's neck exploded in a red mist and it collapsed in a jumble of limbs. Blood spurted from its wounds as it writhed and spasmed in the snow, its arms and legs still pumping and kicking, as its brain caught up to the fact that its spine had been severed.

Nick finally stole a glance to his left where he saw movement earlier and fired into the dark, hoping to get lucky. He racked another round and took off running toward the truck, leaving the pale twisted thing to mewl and shudder, dying in the snow.

Ozzy opened the driver's side truck door and Nick dove inside, slamming the door closed behind him. Nick shoved the shotgun into Ozzy's hand and cranked the key in the ignition. The ignition made a grinding sound as the engine was already on.

Nick was shaking so badly, he could barely grab the wheel. His bloody hand found the gear shift and dropped it into drive.

"Where's mom? Where's Tara?"

Nick couldn't even look at Ozzy. His eyes were pinned

to the two creatures emerging from the dark, running full speed on all fours toward the truck. Large black shapes, covered in dark camouflage and pelts of fur, the size of grizzly bears, barrelling out of the darkness.

"Dad. Where's Mom?"

Nick stole a glance at Ozzy. There was nothing he could say to lessen the blow, and there was no time to say it.

"Put your seatbelt on."

Ozzy complied without a word, pain and grief squeezing his face into a grimace.

Nick hit the gas and the truck jerked forward, out of the rut he dug spinning the tires earlier. Nick slammed the shifter into reverse.

"Dad! Dad!" Ozzy screamed, staring out through the windshield. Nick followed Ozzy's terrified gaze and realized, they were out of time.

The creatures converged on the truck, hitting it head on. The largest one rushed straight at the front grill and slammed its fists into the hood denting the metal. The second creature leapt onto the hood itself, climbing easily over the top of the cab, its sharpened fingernails scratching grooves into the paint as it scrambled into the truck bed.

Nick stomped on the gas pedal and the truck lurched backwards, bouncing over the snow drifts. The creature in the truck bed was pressed into the cab by the sudden change of speed and it roared in frustration.

Glass shattered.

Nick and Ozzy whipped their heads toward the

sound and watched as the creature's narrow head squeezed through the broken rear window.

Ozzy screamed as Nick grabbed the shotgun. He spun in his seat and extended his arm, as he pressed the barrel to the center of the creature's shrieking face and yanked the trigger.

The monster's face imploded in a cataclysmic boom and the power of the blast forced what remained of its body to flop out of sight and into the bed of the truck.

Nick dropped the shotgun into the back seat, the recoil burning a line of pain up his arm and into his shoulder, which would've hurt like a bitch if he had the time to notice. The truck had drifted off line where he imagined the road to be and he cranked the wheel, correcting their trajectory.

The windshield was clear as the truck picked up speed, rolling quickly downhill through the snow, bouncing over the edge of the driveway and toward the road below.

A flicker of movement to his left forced Nick to turn his head at the last moment and catch the dark shape barreling toward him. The driver's side window exploded inward as the creature's bloody face smashed through the glass. Its massive jaws snapped and sprayed Nick with ropy streams of saliva and tendrils of bloody flesh. Nick crushed the gas pedal as he dove away from the shattered window.

The monster's hungry roar filled the cabin and drowned out the screams of the two remaining Jacksons. Snow and trees whipped past as the truck rocketed backwards. There was a flash of sparks as the undercarriage scraped across the asphalt, bounced once and then continued across the narrow road and down the slope of the opposite side.

The creature shifted position, reaching into the cab and grabbed Nick by the front of his coat, its long talon like fingernails digging through the thin material of his parka and piercing flesh. Nick screamed and uselessly swatted at the creature's iron grip.

Nick was ripped toward the driver's door and his head struck the frame opening a bloody gash above his eyes. Pain was replaced by stars for a moment as Nick felt weightless in the truck moving so fast downhill.

Ozzy was pinned to his seat, doing his best to curl into a ball. To hide.

A pine tree struck the passenger side of the truck and the truck spun on its axis, sliding sideways now, smashing into barely concealed boulders and the broken trunks of ancient pines.

The creature groped for Nick again, its claws anchoring into the side of his face, gouging grooves into his flesh and cutting tendons.

Nick opened his mouth to scream and then the truck struck a tree broadside. Suddenly the pressure on Nick's face and throat was gone. The creature disappeared from the driver's side window.

The truck flipped over, spinning and bouncing down the slope, shedding bits of glass and pieces of twisted metal as it dropped and bent and rolled deeper into the darkness.

Ozzy's head slammed into the roof with a gong sound and then the passenger window broke with a sharp crack like ice breaking, starring the glass. The bright pain in his temple was smothered by a blackness so absolute it pulled him into it entirely, like a black hole.

A place where there was no sound. No movement.

Only the dark.

FORTY-FIVE

Ozzy tried to blink but it was difficult. His eyelids seemed to have frozen together. His heartbeat jolted into a higher gear and he opened his mouth to cry out. His head was throbbing and there was pain burning across his chest. Ozzy opened his eyes and found himself dangling from his seatbelt looking down at the plastic dashboard of the truck.

He tried to raise his head and failed. He could see watery sunlight edging into the dark confines of the truck, but no details.

"Dad?" His voice was barely above a whisper and it hurt his throat. He swallowed and tried again with the same result.

He braced himself against the dashboard with his legs, and unclipped his seatbelt. His legs were frozen and stiff, and barely broke his fall. He crumpled to the ceiling of the truck in a heap. The sound of his awkward fall was canon fire in the silence of the winter forest. He scanned the interior of the truck cab, the back seat. Frozen crystals of blood were splashed over the interior, but his father was gone.

Did he leave me?

"Dad?"

His breath smoked in the semi-dark. There was no response.

Ozzy peered through the open passenger window into the forest and saw that the storm had passed. Snow covered every tree and rock in a perfect sheet of white, but the wind had finally died.

After another scan of his surroundings he crawled out of the wreckage and stood next to the truck. He could see a path gouged through the forest slope and with no better option, he began climbing back up to the road.

Slowly his legs warmed up with the exertion and his joints loosened, but his hands and feet felt numb, as did the tip of his nose and the tops of his cheeks. When he touched those parts of his face they didn't feel like flesh. They felt more like leather.

Moving carefully, Ozzy made his way at his own pace up the steep slope. From tree to tree he kept searching the snow covered forest floor for footsteps made by his father.

For a smear of red.

For anything.

Maybe he went for help and would be coming straight back?

Maybe he was thrown from the truck and he's lying somewhere hurt?

The thought forced Ozzy to stop and turn, and scan the forest behind him. He saw only snow covered rocks and trees, and even if his father was hurt, what could he do but go for help?

He trudged on.

More sunlight began to bleed through the tangle of branches as he climbed higher and higher. He reached for a branch the size of his wrist and something moved behind him. Below him.

Thin branches snapped and he could hear something scuttle in the dark.

A rabbit. A squirrel.

Ozzy pressed on, moving quicker, stealing glances over his shoulder as he planted his feet, and looked for his next hand hold as he pulled himself toward the sun, and the road beyond.

Soon he could hear the buzz of tires on asphalt and the spray of slush hitting the shoulder of the road.

Another few feet, another couple of slippery handholds, sliding over ice covered boulders and Ozzy could smell woodsmoke and hear the distant din of conversation.

Level with the road he could see the charred remains of the cabin, and the cluster of emergency vehicles parked in the driveway.

Police, fire and ambulance crews had all arrived, their blue and red emergency lights spinning uselessly in the daylight. First responders milled around the cabin, clustered in groups or standing by themselves, their breath steaming in the frigid air.

Ozzy scrambled to the edge of the road, his hands reaching for the asphalt and then, with a firm grip, struggled to his feet. A man wearing a cream colored cowboy hat and a brown police uniform strode past a group of three paramedics huddled together smoking in a tight circle. He nodded to them as he passed and then trudged on down to the end of the driveway where his Sheriff's cruiser was parked.

Ozzy raised an arm and waved at the officer, his voice still too hoarse to make any meaningful sound.

The Sheriff saw him, he was sure of it. The cop's eyes, even behind the mirrored shades he wore, never left Ozzy's face.

Branches bent and twisted behind Ozzy, as something clawed through the snow. He could hear the chuff of ragged breathing and the grunt of exertion behind him.

Ozzy raised his hand to wave again and the Sheriff lifted his own in reply.

The Sheriff took a step toward the road, pointing at Ozzy. He was yelling something now. Ozzy waved again, smiling. Until he saw the Sheriff screaming, waving his arms, pointing madly.

Not *at* Ozzy.

Behind him.

Ozzy's smile curdled, his ruddy complexion faded to the color of bone.

The Sheriff jogged toward the road as a U-Haul truck

blasted its horn, nearly erasing him from the world. The truck barrelled by so close he could feel the wind on his face, and the half second it took for the truck to clear, he already knew he was too late.

The spot where he saw the boy was empty.

He drew his pistol and charged across the asphalt, slipping over the black ice and kicking through the slush on the opposite side. He scanned the slope, his gun up and aimed downrange.

Trees swayed in the light wind, snow spiralling down from a cobalt blue sky.

He grabbed a tree branch and clamoured down the slope, his boots slipping over the frozen ground.

"Hey kid!" The Sheriff yelled. "Where are you?"

Ozzy lay facedown in the dark, a weight crushed into his back, squeezing every breath out of his lungs. He could hear the Sheriff's call, he could hear the tumble of rocks kicked loose as he made his way down the hill.

He was so close.

Ozzy writhed and struggled, but hands pinned him in an iron grip to the cold ground. Claws scratched at his face and worked their way toward his mouth. Rough fingers pushed past his clenched lips and into his mouth. Fingers that tasted of blood and dirt.

"Kid, answer me!"

Ozzy shifted position and dragged in a ragged breath, and even with the monster's fingers tunnelling deeper into his throat, forcing his mouth open, wider and wider, he forced himself to scream, to signal that he was still there.

He was still alive.

Ozzy could hear the sound of ripping leather as the skin at the corners of his mouth tore. The bones of his jaw creaked and cracked as they dislocated. Ozzy's hands swung wildly, finding the prickly branch of a tree.

Sunlight speared his eyes in the dark as gunfire exploded all around him. Claws were yanked from the inside of his mouth leaving deep grooves in the soft flesh. The painful pressure on his back disappeared replaced with the agonizing shrieks that burrowed into his ears like starving rats.

Thundering footsteps rushed away in the dark getting harder and harder to hear as the Sheriff kept muttering, *"What the hell? What the hell? What the hell?"*

Blood ran warmly down Ozzy's face and from his mouth, but he was comfortable lying there in the snow. His body was warm.

"I need everyone down here now, straight across the road from the cabin, down the slope." The Sheriff hollered into his radio. "I got a kid all cut up over here."

Ozzy could feel hands move over his back and under his shoulder, as the Sheriff gently pressed his fingers into the side of his throat, searching for a pulse.

"Christ, hurry up." The Sheriff yelled again into his microphone.

And then the Sheriff was leaning close to Ozzy, his hot breath inches from his face.

"Hold on, kid." He whispered, "Hold on."

And then to himself, "What the hell was that?" As he shifted his position, and scanned the snowy trees for the creature, he saw it, but still didn't believe what he was seeing was real.

But it *was* real.

And it was not so easy to deter, or to kill.

Ozzy's gaze was angled down the slope, his glazed eye staring into the shadows beneath the canopies of towering pine trees.

He wanted to warn the nice police officer. To say something. But he was so tired, and so warm, and his vision was darkening, curling in at the edges.

The ground rumbled with their footsteps, running on all fours as they charged up the hill through the dark.

He could hear the Sheriff turn and swear and fire his first shot.

The rumbling didn't stop and then the creatures chorus of roars drowned out the screaming of the Sheriff and the last few pistol cracks.

Ozzy couldn't move, his tired limbs were lined with concrete. His wheezing breath crackled out of his crushed throat with the sound of crinkling cellophane.

He whispered a prayer.

He prayed there would be no more pain.

He prayed he would see his family soon.

The Sheriff's boots skidded on the icy ground and scrambled out of view. He heard the heavy wet thud of the cop's body as it was tackled to the ground. Ozzy heard the thrash of the Sheriff's limbs kicking up snow and shaking the low branches, and then the gurgling choke of his dying breath.

The strange chittering language replaced the

monsters' battle cry. Long black talons ripped into the snowy ground as the stink of their rancid bodies flooded into the dimly lit space.

Ozzy heard faraway voices. Calling out, coming closer, as they slipped and slid down an icy slope. Guns out, as they searched for their colleague. Their friend.

As they stumbled straight into a trap.

And he heard their screams.

When they came, they sounded muffled and far away, as Ozzy's world collapsed to a shrinking pinpoint until the last glimmer of sunlight is smothered by a tide of crushing darkness.

ACKNOWLEDGMENTS

A lot of people helped shape the book you just read. Not least of all, are my amazing beta readers who took the time to read through my early drafts and help me create a book worth sharing with the world. I am eternally grateful to all of you.

Seth Wimmer
Erika Poynter
Danielle Yeager
Elisa Destiny Lott
Milt Theodossiou
Jenni Leonard
Sammi Dyer
Sophie Griffiths
Brien Feathers
Evelyn Arfeuille
Phil Baker
Heather Larson
Trista Jarrard
Chandra Marie
Kennedy Linne Keown
Elise Wilson
Dan Lawson

Liz Priest Wallace

Leigh Kenny

Kaylie Jarrell

As well as the entire Books of Horror Facebook group - you are all amazing!

ABOUT THE AUTHOR

Patrick McNulty is an author, screenwriter, husband and father to three amazing children. He lives in Ontario, Canada.

FREE BOOK

I write pretty fast and new releases are coming out all the time. So to stay in the loop and get some free books along the way, check out my website and get a **FREE** digital copy of **THE BLOOD SINGER** just for stopping by.

www.patrickmcnulty.ca

Printed in Great Britain
by Amazon

22097332R00159